To Save a Bad Guy

SARAH GALLER

Contents

Chapter 1

"I just don't understand why you read that junk," he told me with a smirk, sliding the comic book out of my hands and flipping through its colorful pages just to annoy me. "And you've marked every single page involving him? That's just weird."

To point this out, my brother held up one of the dog-eared pages and gestured toward the thin, dark haired character standing in one of the panels. He was holding a gun in his hand and using it against the comic's heroes.

"Give it back," I muttered grumpily, yanking it out of his shaking hands. He was laughing so hard he didn't have the strength to stop me.

"You are aware that he's the villain, right?" Joe asked me as I rose from the living room couch and headed toward my bedroom in the hopes of escaping his cruel remarks. "Why are you so obsessed with him?"

Normally, I would have slammed the door in his face and escaped to the welcoming world of my favorite series but this was the third time this week that Joe had bugged me about this. I couldn't stand it anymore.

Feeling my cheeks burn at what I was about to say, I turned my head far enough to glare at him and spoke. "Because if you'd gone through what he went through, you'd act the same way." Actually, Joe would probably act worse.

"Stockholm Syndrome!" my idiot brother called as I gave up and locked him out. Joe wasn't a bad guy, he was just too immature to put himself in other people's shoes. He'd grow out of it eventually, I hoped.

"He has a point though," I muttered under my breath as I sank into the fabrics of my bed. Anyone who looked around at my posters and book collection would know that I cared about the villain of this series a little too much. His face was plastered all over my walls.

"I wonder how much money I would have saved if I hadn't become a fan of his." As I placed the comic back on the shelf with its twenty-four siblings I slid my fingers over the various covers.

"Manica: The Moon Revenge." "Manica: The Adventures of Jala and Ace." "Manica: The Mysterious Stranger."

They were all great books, don't get me wrong, but the most worn book in the series, the one I'd read five times in a row when I'd first bought it, was the one titled "The Origins of Dark".

Dark was the name of the series' most notorious villain, the wealthy, charismatic playboy with a dark past and an unpredictable personality. He became famous for being over the top and acting sweet to cover up his dark intentions.

When I first heard about Dark I didn't think much of him. He seemed like a stereotypical villain and I wasn't really the type to go for the bad boy since I knew guys like that would most definitely cheat on me. It wasn't until I stumbled across the origin book, which I'd found on sale for five dollars, that I started to care about him.

The tale went that Dark used to work with the story's main characters and he hadn't been that bad of a guy. He had a few issues, sure, as he'd been forced to live with his apparently insane grandmother and had an awful boss but other than that he had been somewhat likeable. He had always struck me as the type to cover up his insecurities with humor and that was why he'd become so popular with readers.

The only reason Dark became so evil was because his wife ended up dying and his "friends" later turned against him because he was so unstable from it.

Seeing so much happiness and sorrow come out of the same man, one who everyone hated and loved because of his villainy, struck something in my heart. I'd never been sure what it was about him that turned my heart but whatever it was had been enough to make me fall for him.

...Well, as much as you can fall for a fictional character.

One thing led to another and I became obsessed with the entire series, spending more money on merchandise than I should have. Infatuation can do that to you. And here I thought I was a logical girl.

Anyway, that was why I was rethinking my life choices as I stared at Dark's cartoon face and bright colored attire. Honestly, he wasn't even that handsome in my eyes. His looks were an acquired taste, I think. It was just his personality that drew me in.

"I need to stop thinking about you and live my own life in the real world," I told him, jokingly pointing a finger at the poster. "I'm graduating this year and have to actually fall in love with a real man."

I might have kept talking to the piece of paper like a madman if Joe hadn't passed by and yelled my name, letting me know that he could hear my weird, one sided discussion.

Sighing, I yelled for the fool to go away and decided that, from now on, all conversations would continue in my head. "Dark, I am sorry for everything that happened to you...even though you are fiction al...," I thought to myself. "And I wish that the writers hadn't been so against you. They really threw every evil plot device imaginable at you."

If the authors hadn't already known that Dark was going to become the villain, the story definitely would have played out differently and he would have been fine. He might have even ended up nicer than the other main characters.

But, alas, that was not how stories worked.

"I wish your wife hadn't died," I whispered mournfully. They hadn't shown her in the books but since Dark's daughter had been so nice the mother must have been sweet too. "If she'd lived, I don't think you would have lost your mind the way you did."

Chest rising and falling, I raised my cell to my face and scrolled through some of the videos I'd collected from the cartoon show based on the comics. Dark had been a side character in it and I'd memorized all the parts he was in.

...Goodness. I really was obsessed, wasn't I?

"I suppose I should start deleting these." It would be the first step to ending my addiction. But...Nah.

I shoved the phone in my pocket. I could always do it later. After all, it wasn't like I was going into college tomorrow or anything. I still had one more year left.

"Yes," I sighed, lying flat on the bed and running my fingers through my straight, blonde hair. Tomorrow. I could do it tomorrow. Right now I'd just allow myself to indulge in the thought that Dark was real and deserved my sympathy.

As I lay there, letting my mind run through the events of the most recent episode I'd watched of the show, a sudden thought came to mind, one I'd never allowed myself to think before.

"What if I had been Dark's wife?"

The question came as a shock even to me. Sure, I'd loved Dark as a character but I'd never thought of my obsession as a crush. The thought of marrying him had never crossed my mind.

But now that I was on the subject...What would it be like? Would I have been able to save him from himself? Even if I didn't marry him and just helped him avoid those traumatic events in his life would he have stayed good? And would that have been enough to keep the main characters from killing him at the end of the series?

I shouldn't have thought about it. "What ifs" are never good, even if they're about something that never happened.

But it was fun to think about.

So, as I lay on my mattress with my eyes closed and hair splayed across my pillow, I daydreamed about what I could have done. During that time, all my worries seemed to fade away and it was almost like I was transported to the magical world of Manica itself. I could almost taste the fresh air and warm breeze.

Of course, all comfort vanished as soon as I opened my eyes and looked up to find that, instead of my bedroom ceiling, a blue sky hung above my head and I could see a large moon dangling among the clouds. It looked way bigger than our moon on Earth.

That's when the panic set in and I sat up, forgetting how to breath as I spun around to study the grassy field I was sitting in. My lovely bed was gone and replaced with soil and my house was nowhere to be seen.

"Wha...?" This wasn't good.

As I crawled to my feet, trying to keep a level head and keep in mind that this was probably a dream, I looked around to try and get my bearings. A quick scan revealed that there was a small town at the end of this field, behind me, and I could see a few blurry people and cars passing by which meant I could probably ask someone for help.

But...that moon. It was just so wrong and out of place. It didn't belong on Earth...which meant this was not my home.

A quick, painful pinch on my left arm also revealed that this was not a dream and that was enough to send spasms through my legs, making them threaten to drop out from under me and never work again.

I was in another world! I wasn't dreaming! And...

"Are you doing okay?"

My head jerked toward the unfamiliar, deep voice and, with it, my heart dropped into my useless legs when I saw who it was.

Standing before me with a grocery bag dangling from his hands was Dark! His dark, Brazilian face was scrunched up in confusion. He must have witnessed my arrival.

His dark chocolate hair and tight, blue shirt looked identical to my favorite poster of him but he didn't have the same dark look in his eyes. They seemed brighter, less plotting and manipulative. It was similar to how he'd looked at the beginning of his origin story before all the awful things happened.

He must have been passing by on the street and spotted me freaking out over here. How kind of him to check on me.

...What had he asked me about again? I'd forgotten.

"Hey." Hesitantly, as though he was worried that I might be dangerous or unstable, he took a step forward and held out a hand to steady me. "Are you okay? Do you need to go to a hospital or something?"

I'd always hated when the girls in stories would clam up and act like rag dolls when they see a guy. I found characters like that super annoying, especially when they were normally level headed. But being in this situation and knowing it wasn't a dream just sent all rational thoughts out the window and all I could do was stare at him with my mouth slightly ajar.

After not receiving an answer, Dark looked over his shoulder, probably in the hopes that someone else would take me off his hands, then he shrugged and grabbed my arm, snapping me out of my daze.

"I'll take you to a hospital," he informed me and began to drag me through the field, keeping his grip firm just in case I fell over or something.

As I allowed myself to be pulled my stupid brain started formulating a plan. If this truly was real and my wish really had come true, maybe...just maybe, I could actually do what I'd joked about earlier.

I didn't plan to marry him, obviously, but if I could become his friend...If I could prepare him for all the disappointment he'd face in the future...

Maybe I could keep him from going insane.

Maybe I could rescue Dark from becoming the villain.

Chapter 2

"What's your name? Do you have a family I can call?" Dark asked me as we walked down the street. Some of the people who passed us gave him a friendly wave or a funny grin which made it abundantly clear that this was a small town where everyone knew everybody.

As we walked, I couldn't help but focus on how warm his hand felt as it gripped my arm. He looked and felt so real and it was strange. It was similar to the sensation one felt when meeting a celebrity in real life, like the person belonged on a screen and was out of place in your world.

Clearing my throat and keeping myself focused on the present, I answered his question as clearly as I could. "My name's Mary. I...am an orphan." Saying that would be way easier than explaining that I came from an alternate reality where he was a villain in a made up world.

"Orphan, huh?" He smirked at that, finally showing part of that snarky personality he'd had onscreen. He was probably thinking about his own situation.

His father had died when he was young and his mother abandoned him on his grandmother's doorstep before disappearing. Based on his age right now, I would guess that he was still living with her now.

"Yeah. I...I don't really want to talk about it, if that's okay with you." Goodness, I was good at lying. Maybe I'd learned it from watching him.

"Sure. Whatever. Do you still want to go to the hospital or will you be okay?"

His actions didn't match his words since he was still holding my wrist.

"Um...No. I think I'm okay...though I don't have anywhere to go." It was true and I did my best to sound lonely and pitiable. My plan was that if he helped me, it would give me an opportunity to become an acquaintance of his and keep an eye on him.

If the universe was giving me this one chance to save him I was not going to throw it away no matter how many lies I had to weave.

"Oh. Sorry."

Ha! He didn't sound sorry at all. He was just trying to figure out what to do with me now. Well, I wouldn't let him off that easily. "What's your name?" I managed to ask, leaning toward him slightly as I spoke.

Dark raised an eyebrow, then chuckled. "Derek Hacket."

"What?"

"Hmm?"

Shoot! I should have kept my mouth shut. Of course Dark wouldn't be his real name. It wasn't even a cool name. Panicking, I tried to switch back to my calm personality but it was long gone. "O...oh. Cool."

My smooth demeanor had left me and was replaced with my natural awkwardness which I didn't want anyone to witness, especially my idol.

Words could not describe the calm I felt when he merely laughed quietly and turned away again, still grinning. "I guess. Mary's fine too...I guess."

There he went again, hesitantly being nice. After years of studying him I had a theory that he secretly wanted to act kind but was just too lazy or shy to do it. Seeing it in action now just made him seem even cuter...not that I cared about such things. I was just here to save him from his fate.

"I really hate to ask you but..." I had to do this or he'd leave and I might never get to see him again. I might even be sent back to Earth. "Would it be possible for me to stay at your house tonight? I don't have anywhere to go, you see, and..." As the words spilled out from between my lips I noticed my lisp start to reveal itself and clamped my mouth shut before I could embarrass myself further.

Now I just had to wait for his answer.

He clearly wanted to say no. There was no doubt about that. His lips were pressed together tightly and he was squinting, as though weighing the pros and cons. Then with the right side of his mouth curling upwards evilly, he nodded, releasing my arm at the same time.

"Sure. I'm sure my grandmother wouldn't mind."

My face lit up. "Really?" That was surprising.

"Of course." Still grinning, he gestured toward a small, wooden house at the end of the street and nodded at it. "But we only have two bedrooms and she doesn't like sharing."

"Oh, I can sleep on the floor," I interjected eagerly, thrilled that my plan was actually working. What were the odds?

"Good." Derek chuckled again before leading me forward.

I might have acted thrilled as we walked but as soon as he chuckled like that, with such an evil grin, I started to feel suspicious. Why was he so willing to let me, a complete stranger, into his home? Once the thought popped into my head, I frowned. He was probably up to something. If it was anyone other than him, I would have booked it because of that. Curse my obligation to keep him safe!

His house looked more like a wooden shack with a picket fence and dying grass from the outside but, once he opened the door and led me inside, it looked more like an expensive home. All the walls were painted white and the furniture was a soft red, reminding me of Valentine's Day decorations.

The back door we entered led straight into the living room. There was a bathroom across from us and a bedroom off to the left. I had to assume that the hallway running past the bedroom farther left led to the kitchen as I could hear some clanging of pots and pans coming from it.

"Grandma! Come here!" Derek yelled after slamming the door and pushing past me, acting as though I wasn't here. If I wasn't so nervous I might have felt a bit miffed at his actions.

Now if I though Dark was scary then the short, grey haired woman who rounded the corner was the devil. Her darting eyes were shining with deceit and hatred and as soon as they moved my way, I felt a shiver run down my back.

"What is that?" she asked as she shot the same look of distaste toward her grandson. "I thought I told you not to bring your girlfriends here."

Oh no. I couldn't keep myself from rubbing my hands together nervously. Was she going to kick me out?

"She's not my girlfriend." He grimaced, which hurt my feelings a little bit. "She's just some homeless girl who needs a place to stay for the night."

Well, he wasn't wrong.

The old woman's voice lowered a little as she leaned toward the young man. "This isn't a charity, Derek." Her voice reminded me of a witch. "Besides, we don't have room."

"I can sleep on the floor!" I offered meekly, waving slightly to get her attention, which I immediately regretted. Her eyes were shooting daggers.

The grandma looked me over more thoroughly this time from my bland, dirty blonde hair to the long black shirt and baggy pants hiding my unimpressive figure. I wasn't insecure about my body but knew it didn't live up to either world's high standards.

"Very well." She finally smiled and it was not pretty. "She can stay here but," she poked Derek's chest, "she's going to stay in your room."

His eyes widened. "What? But I—"

"You brought her in here, you'll take care of her. This isn't a hotel." She said before wrinkling her nose and returning to the kitchen where more banging ensued, louder this time.

I didn't want to look at Derek. I could already sense that he was growing annoyed and definitely didn't want to share his living space with some strange girl he'd taken pity on. Sure enough, when I looked at him he was intentionally avoiding my gaze. Finally, after staring down the wall for a while, he rubbed the back of his neck and pointed to the small bedroom on the left. "I have a bunk bed. You sleep on top."

Well, at least it wasn't the floor.

Chapter 3

Feeling slightly nervous but mainly excited about being in my favorite villain's bedroom, I crept in a bit too slowly and peeked inside. Of course, it was dark but once he turned on the light I got to see just how pitiful the place was.

A lone bunk bed leaned against the wall to my right, its sheets dark black which definitely gave the room a cheery atmosphere. On the wall to the left was a closet, likely full of his clothes and little else based on how many different outfits he'd worn in the comics. And on the far wall was a completely empty dresser.

I'd had no idea Dark was such a minimalist. That or maybe he was too poor to afford anything.

"I'm a minimalist," he explained as though he could read my thoughts. "You're not afraid of the dark, are you?"

I shook my head before realizing that there were no windows in this room. How spooky.

"Good."

"I don't have nightmares either!" I added, raising my hand excitedly. I didn't realize how childish I sounded until he shot me an 'Are you kidding me?' look and I dropped my arm as quick as I could.

"Sorry." I would have excused this attitude as being nervous from the wild day but, honestly, I had always been like this. I was awkward and quiet when I first met people but as soon as I got comfortable I would get ten times weirder. It tended to ruin any potential friendships I attempted to create in high school.

After making it quite clear that he was not impressed, Derek started messing around with the bed sheets before turning to me. "Just don't be loud or anything. If I fail my test because of you I'll..."

I backed away slightly as his slightly annoyed tone increased but he managed to stop himself from making any threats and turned away, visibly calming himself down with deep breaths. "Sorry. I won't do anything. This test is just really important to me."

"What's it for?" I asked, my eyes going wide with genuine curiosity. The comics never talked about his college life. I only got to see him after he was married and somewhat successfully working on the moon's space station.

It took Derek a moment to respond but when he did his eyes seemed to light up a little bit and lost the protective glare they normally had. "Do you really want to know?"

"Of course!" Please, just tell me! I have no life and therefore thrive off of yours!

"Well, I'm applying for a job in the Hikarius Company. If my test scores are high enough, they might even promote me to the moon station in a couple years."

"That's exciting," I said politely, my mind already rewinding to all the events I'd seen play out up there. "Just be sure to keep an eye on your family while you're up there."

"...What?"

"Shoot!" I slammed both hands over my stupid mouth and backed away, mentally punching myself for being so stupid. Now was not the time to give random warnings. I had to establish myself as a trustworthy acquaintance first.

"I mean, if you're gonna be up there all the time you should make sure to check up on your family down here sometimes, right?" I giggled nervously to hide how much of an idiot I was.

Derek just frowned again and scrunched his eyebrows together. "That's kind of a given."

"Of course. Ha ha." I want to die.

I had no idea what this girl's deal was. All I knew was that by bringing her into my home for a night or two, my stupid grandma would quit hitting me for a couple of days. My back could only take so many bruises and I couldn't have the pain distracting me from my schooling.

Pity the girl was such a weirdo, though. What had she said her name was again? Mary? Huh. That was my second to last ex's name. What a creepy coincidence. That ex had been awful.

I was just beginning to reach that point between wake and sleep when she suddenly yelped above my head. Obviously, it jerked me out of my tired state and made me sit up abruptly. I was lucky I didn't hit my head on the top of the bunk when I did so.

I thought she said she didn't have nightmares.

I was beginning to think it was just her adjusting to the bed until it happened again, louder this time.

Seriously? Tonight of all nights?

My first instinct was to shake her awake so that she'd stop being so ... loud but that second scream sounded seriously concerning. After the fourth yell she started thrashing around and I began to wonder if she was going to hurt herself.

"Hey..." It took a lot of convincing but I finally managed to drag myself out of bed and, with even more convincing, shook her arm slightly. I tried to be gentle but it was tough with all of her moving around. "Hey. Wake up!"

For a moment all was still and silent, then she suddenly sat up effortlessly like a ghost and grabbed the front of my shirt. I hate to admit it but I did feel a twinge of fear when she yanked me closer to her face and stared at me with unblinking eyes.

"I can't," she whispered in a deep, desperate voice before shutting her eyes and collapsing onto the pillow, sleeping as though nothing had happened.

...Wow.

I should've just taken the beatings.

Chapter 4

When I awoke it was pitch black, making me believe it was still the middle of the night. I must have covered my bedroom window last night but...why couldn't I remember doing it? I couldn't remember doing anything yesterday. All I could remember was...

Oh no! I wasn't in my bedroom!

Gradually running my fingers around the bed, searching for my familiar pillows and stuffed animal, everything came flooding back. As my hands made contact with the top of the bunk bed, everything that had happened yesterday ran through my mind like a distorted flashback.

It took me a few minutes to think about it, then a second realization struck me. I had fallen asleep on the top bunk. So why could I feel that same bunk hanging above my head?

"Am I..."

Taking a deep breath, I turned away from the wall I was facing and looked to see if anyone else was lying in the bed.

Someone was.

Still sleeping, his hair messy and shirt wrinkled, was Dark or, rather, Derek. Why was I sleeping next to him? Had I started to sleep walk? But I never did at home.

Now, I want to pause for a second and be honest. I am sure that most girls would have loved to be in my position in that moment. Dark was the rugged, bad boy type, probably what many girls dreamed about. But, at that moment, thoughts of marrying him and being romantic were the farthest things from my mind. At the time, I just cared about protecting him like a sister or friend. So lying next to him only made my heart jump out of fear, not love.

Priorities came first. If I had crawled in while I was asleep, maybe he didn't know. And, based on how he'd acted yesterday, when he did wake up he'd probably be angry to see me in here with him so I needed to sneak out before that happened.

It took a lot of concentration to slowly inch my legs, one after the other, out from under the blankets. Unfortunately for me, I was up against the wall which meant I'd need to climb over Derek in order to get out. How on earth had I climbed in here last night?

I was right above him, one leg on either side of his body, ready to leap onto the floor and escape, when he woke up.

I was expecting him to get mad or shove me off but, as he slowly rubbed his eyes and looked up at me wearily, all he did was give a small chuckle.

"I know I'm handsome but isn't it a bit early to jump me?" he asked, still tired but amused.

How dare he?! "Don't flatter yourself," I muttered before finally freeing myself from the awkward position I was in. As I brushed myself off and felt around in my pockets for my phone, I inwardly applauded myself for responding so quickly without stumbling over my words. For me, that was an accomplishment.

I wanted to check what time it was but, unfortunately, my phone didn't seem to be working. The screen stayed black no matter what I did, which was annoying. Maybe it's battery couldn't work in this world or something.

"Do you guys have electricity?" I started to ask before remembering that he'd turned on a light earlier today. Maybe they had electricity but weren't advanced enough for cell phones. I hadn't bothered to notice such things in the book.

"Why? Do you need to call somebody?" Derek asked as he stumbled out of the bed at a far slower pace than I had. "And you're asking about that instead of what happened last night?"

My eyes popped out of my head. "What happened last night?!?" So I hadn't been sleep walking?

After running both hands through his dark hair to make it look presentable, he gave me a one over, then smirked like the villain I wouldn't let him become. "Maybe I shouldn't tell you."

"Maybe you should!"

"Okay. Okay." He laughed. "You kept having nightmares and would only stop screaming when I touched you so, after the fifth time, I gave up and just brought you down here..." He pointed to the bottom bunk. "So I could finally get some sleep."

"Oh. Sorry." How embarrassing. And how unusual. I never had nightmares at home. Maybe it was another side effect of the world changing thing. I wonder what I'd been dreaming about.

"Good thing it was only for one night, right?" he asked and stepped toward the door, preparing for school.

Realization struck me as he brushed past. He only planned to let me stay over once. Now what should I do? I didn't know anybody here. And...

"Wait!" I whimpered and grabbed his arm, embarrassed at how pathetic I sounded but unable to come up with a better idea. "Please, I have nowhere else to go."

"Not my problem."

"I can pay rent! I can get a job! I can—"

"Deal."

"...What?" Why had he agreed so quickly?

Derek smiled and brushed off my arm. "If you pay rent and keep grandma off my back, I'll let you sleep in my room. I'll even hold your hand if you like," he added mockingly, a cheeky grin on his face.

My face fell as I realized he was using me. He really was a jerk. How was I supposed to save this guy from becoming the villain when he was already like this?

"But if I tell you to leave, you'll have to go without a fight, understood?" His face told me that if I made one wrong move, I'd be back on the streets in a minute.

Well, it was better than nothing. At least I'd have a place to stay. Gulping and chewing on the insides of my mouth, I held out my hand. "Deal."

"Good," he said before ignoring my offer and stepping into the living room, yawning dramatically as he went. I had to keep myself from kicking him. What a piece of work! If he wasn't such a sympathetic character and if I wasn't trapped in this world for who knew how long, I would have left him right then and there.

Chapter 5

His grandma had already left by the time we came out for breakfast so I'd dodged a bullet there but the next issue was how to find a job, which would be hard since I technically wasn't an official citizen of this world. What kind of paperwork would I need to fill out here?

I believe Derek started to get a little creeped out by my clinginess because he drew a line with a glare when I followed him into the closet, unaware that he was planning to change out of his pajamas.

"Do you mind if I follow you into town on your way to school?" I asked meekly while watching him assemble his backpack full of books. "I won't go in with you. I promise."

The guy shot me a look too hard for me to read, then hefted his pack over his shoulder. "You're really lucky you ran into me and not some creep. A normal person wouldn't tolerate you like this."

"I know." I honestly did know. I normally wasn't like this in the real world...but this wasn't the real world. In here I could do whatever I wanted. He couldn't understand how much of a dream come true this was for me. "Don't worry. I'll go job hunting as soon as you leave."

"Have a good day!" I called as Derek entered the gate to his college. As soon as I spoke, he covered his face in exasperation and hurried to the front door, weaving between his fellow students as they shot amused looks my way.

It wasn't until I started walking back down the street by myself that I realized how much I'd looked like a wife or mother sending their child off. How humiliating for Dark.

Oh well. I had other things to worry about, like finding a job.

You'd think that when someone enters a magical land they'd fall into an adventure where they were the hero and got to tell everyone else what to do. Instead, I had to go job searching on my second day.

The breeze blowing through the streets was a bit cold and since all I had on was the blue shirt and jeans I'd come in with, I had to rub my hands over my arms to keep warm. If Derek didn't snag all my money I'd need to use what was left to buy some new clothes. Luckily, until then, I could still blend in with my normal clothing. The styles weren't that different here.

Now that I'd mentioned it, Manica was very parallel to Earth on many levels. All of the stores I passed were ones you'd normally see in a small town: clothing, grocery, convenience, bars, etc. The cars that sped by were sleeker than normal but seemed Earth-like enough. The only difference was that not everyone was on a cellphone, though I did spot a couple men using headphones. Parallels like these would make adjusting to this world much easier.

"I suppose I could apply at all of these places," I told myself as I traversed the lines of stores, trying to look on the bright side. "I could get lucky—"

Suddenly, I stopped considering my options and ran toward a small bar off to my right. The building was painted black and red and the round, blinking ad on top read "Odette's".

"You've got to be kidding me," I whispered, feeling my legs go numb with excitement. Odette's? The Odette's?

It didn't take me more than a second to charge inside.

Odette, the owner of this bar, was a main character in the Manica Series. She wasn't a soldier like most of the characters but always took part in the action. If I could choose any ally in this world, it would be her.

The inside was somewhat dark and the round tables were full of young men and women, each drinking multi colored drinks, and there was a small band of robots playing electronic music off to my right.

But there, standing behind the bar at the end of the room, was Odette.

Her hair had been painted a bright red to match the bar decorations and her dark makeup made her look more like a celebrity than an employee. Covering her body was a long, black shirt and some red shorts, which fit her rather snugly. Her dark shoes were tied with scarlet laces and looked so unique that I was feeling slightly envious.

If I recalled correctly, she was supposed to be in her early thirties and used to date Dark, so the pair would usually go back and forth between friendship and hatred over time. She would be perfect to talk to about Derek.

"Can I help you?" Odette asked as I walked toward her. Her voice was sophisticated and smooth as sugar. Just hearing her speak brought back so many memories and I immediately felt comfortable around her.

"I'm here to ask..." Realization dawned on me when I realized how odd it would be to ask her about Derek when we'd just met. "I need a job. Are you hiring?"

She looked me over, placing a finger on her chin to let me know she was considering it. "Have you worked at a bar before?" she asked as her eyes trailed from my face to my legs, probably to assess how I would look in a uniform.

I blushed. "No. But I did work at an ice cream shop for two years."

"Hmm." Her snake-like grin told me she enjoyed making me wait. No wonder she and Derek got along. "I was thinking about hiring a new waitress anyway. Come into the back and I'll see what I can do. Joe!"

I jumped when she called my brother's name over my shoulder but she was only ordering one of the robots to come and watch the bar for her. As soon as it arrived I couldn't help but stare at it.

It was very cute, its metal abdomen round and its two fingered arms only big enough to pick up bottles and receive cash. Its head also barely reached the top of the counter, which made it look even cuter. When it realized I was looking at it, it blinked twice at me in before squinting for a while, something I assumed was meant to represent a smile since it didn't have a nose or mouth.

"Come with me, hun," Odette said, gently pulling me through a side door into the back room where a dresser full of makeup and a mirror were waiting. After sitting me down, she left me in front of the mirror and headed into a small walk-in fridge to find something.

"Wow." I couldn't help but tinker with the mounds of makeup in front of me. They ranged from blushes to eye liner to dark, dark eyeshadow which I assumed she used to create that smoky eye of hers. I hadn't worn makeup since grade nine so this would be fun to try again.

"Now." Odette exited the fridge carrying a likely very cold uniform which consisted of tight, black leather pants and a long sleeved, red shirt. Since I was expecting something worse it didn't scare me in the least. "You'll need to wear this and do your makeup every day before coming in to work since I'm notorious for my pretty girls and cute robots." She cringed even as she said it. "It's the only thing that keeps me ahead of my competition."

"Okay." I chuckled, ignoring how similar this aspect was to the real world. "Are you sure I'm pretty enough, though?"

The woman rolled her eyes. "You are very pretty. Plus, makeup is our best friend. Once I'm done with you, you'll bring in lots of business...I hope."

I giggled, looking forward to it.

This would be my very first makeover. Take that, stupid brother who said I was never pretty enough to get ahead in life.

Chapter 6

"I hate to ask this," I began as she applied powders to my face and dark lines to my eyes. "But why did you hire me so quickly?" It seemed a bit...odd.

"Oh." The woman chuckled as she drew a line across my eyebrow to make it more defined. "I saw you and Derek walk past earlier. Figured if he was letting you be seen in public with him then you must be somewhat interesting."

"Oh? He doesn't bring other girls into public?" What exactly did she mean by public? It sounded pretty shady.

"I haven't seen a girl come out of his house before," Odette explained hurriedly. "Sorry. I tend to say one thing and mean another. It means that you're special, I suppose, since he never lets girls into his house."

Probably 'cause he wouldn't want a girl he liked to be around his devilish grandmother. "So that's the only reason?"

"Yes..." After saying it, her grin faltered and she caved. "And, honestly, you're the first person in a month who's applied. I don't really have any other options."

"Putting a 'Help Wanted' sign out might help."

"A what?"

"A help—." Did this world not have help wanted signs or was Odette just a ditz? Shrugging inwardly, I brushed it off. "Never mind. It doesn't matter now that I'm here."

"Right." With that, Odette stepped away from me and admired her work. "You can look in the mirror now."

The face that greeted me in the reflection was similar to mine but more toned with bigger eyes and brighter lips. I hated to admit it but I really did look prettier. Plus, the outfit I was wearing really complimented my body type. I loved it!

"So." The artist grinned shyly. "What do you think?"

As I ran a hand through my hair, which she'd spent twenty minutes curling, I couldn't help but allow my face to light up. "I love it."

This made Odette smile even more. "I'm glad. Now." She switched to a business-like attitude. "Time to teach you your job...I'm sure my customers will love you."

I'd read a lot of books in my time. Granted, a lot of them were comic books but still that was a lot of reading. But, even after all that, I'd have to say that this book was, without a doubt, the most boring one I had ever read.

"Are you ever going to put that dictionary down and start eating?" one of my three friends asked, pulling the book out of my hands and gesturing toward the full cafeteria plate before me.

Grimacing, I shoved the food toward him before snatching my reading material back. "I need to finish this in order to pass."

"Or you could stop being lame and come to Odette's with us," one of the other boys suggested. "James told us there's a new girl working there and she's quite--."

"I'm good," I muttered, leaning back in my chair and pretending to sleep just to show him how much I cared.

Unfortunately, the third boy figured out why I was acting this way and chuckled. "You and Odette broke up years ago. I don't get why you keep avoiding the place?"

"Plus, now that Jane's gone you can go wherever you want," the third one added, referring to my ex.

That bugged me. It had only been two days since the break up and he was already mentioning it? What was wrong with him?

Then I chuckled to myself. If only they knew about that small blonde hiding away in my house. That would give the school enough gossip to last a week. "Maybe after the test," I finally answered, making the boys breathe sighs of relief. They apparently liked bringing me along because it attracted girls.

"I got a job today," she informed me as I made the bed, using both sheets for one bunk this time so that neither of us would have to worry about the other being a blanket hog.

"Good." I didn't really care how she got the money, just so long as she brought it here. As soon as I'd told grandma about the rent she'd stopped complaining and hadn't been around since. I was so glad I took the chance and let this girl in here, even if I did need to sleep next to her. Sharing a bed was preferable to a beating.

At least she seemed nervous about sharing the bed. It was fun to watch her pace and fiddle with her necklace when she thought I wasn't looking. It kind of felt like having a small, annoying wife that you didn't care about in the slightest...so more like a sister, I guess.

"Get in," I ordered, pressed one finger against the light switch. It didn't take her more than two seconds to dive in and claim the spot by the wall, which seemed a bit odd but I didn't care and just climbed in after her.

"Don't worry," I said, noticing how much she was shaking. "I won't do anything to you." My standards weren't that low.

"Okay. Good."

After staring at her back for a few funny seconds, I held out my hand to her, knowing she'd hate this next part. "Hand."

"...What?"

I smirked. "Give me your hand."

"Why?" Her eyes were wide with an unnatural fear. Did she not grow up with any brothers?

Sighing, I waved my hand around, refusing to stop until she gave in. "You would only stop screaming if I was touching you last night so I've decided that if we hold hands all night you won't have nightmares and I won't need to wake up every hour on the hour."

"Okay," she whispered and began to pull out her own hand before hesitating once more. "But won't our hands be numb when we wake up tomorrow."

I sighed, started to grow genuinely annoyed. "Just hold my hand so I can go to sleep!"

"Okay." All hesitation gone, she quickly wrapped her fingers around mind and turned away again, this time for good.

I couldn't help but notice how much her warm, small hands were shaking within mine. As I stared at our intertwined fingers, slowly lowering my head onto the pillow, a small laugh escaped my lips.

"What is it?" she asked, her words muffled by the pillow she had planted her face in.

"It's just cute, that's all," I said, holding up our hands before dropping them and closing my eyes. "Good night. Don't have nightmares."

"I'll try not to."

Chapter 7

I couldn't help but notice that the bar was far more crowded now than it had been a week ago when I'd first been hired. Maybe there was a special holiday coming up or something, though Odette hadn't mentioned anything.

As I stood behind the bar, washing some unusually shaped and hard to clean bottles, I occasionally glanced up at the small robots who managed to play different songs every day. They weren't like animatronics, which would just sing over and over and make the same motions until they broke. These ones could react to people and voices and would answer specific questions if asked. This world really was more advanced than ours, if even by a mere ten years.

"How are things with Derek going?" Odette suddenly snapped me out of my daze, bringing me back to the present. It was a relief to have a distraction since I didn't want to think about the world I'd left behind and the parents I hadn't even said good bye to.

"...Things are going fine. I haven't been hurt yet," I answered with my cheery, customer-service voice. I was referring to his grandmother who, according to the books, used to be very violent before...uh...she died.

Unfortunately, Odette was picturing something very different. "Has he threatened you or anything?" she asked, resting a hand on my arm protectively. "If he has, I can—."

"No, no." Seeing her act like my mother made me giggle. "I was referring to his grandmother. Derek's been fine." Though he still didn't like me all that much. He was very good at tolerating my presence, though. I also apparently hadn't been screaming in the night, which was a relief.

"Okay, good. But if anything bad happens you just let me know. Don't want to see you ended up in an abusive relationship you can't get out of," she said with a tone that reflected wounds of her past.

As I watched her turn back and start mixing a pink and blue drink, I considered telling her that Dark and I weren't in a relationship. But then I'd have to explain that I was paying rent to live with them and that would mean explaining where my family was and I didn't want to get caught in a lie. So, I stayed quiet.

But, since she thought we were dating, there'd be no harm in asking some questions now. If I was going to find his future wife and prevent her death I needed to start an investigation. If only the comics had used a more specific label than "wife".

"Uh...how many girls has Derek dated?" She could have been an ex that he got back together with.

Odette glanced at me, then smiled sympathetically. "You don't need to worry about such things."

"I know but...If I can find out what they did wrong I'll know what to avoid."

More sympathy. She really thought I was lovesick, didn't she? "I didn't really know him before we started dating. I was still recovering from my first husband, you see, but after Derek and I dated and broke up I'd say he's dated maybe..." She paused and tried to calculate. "Eight girls? Maybe nine? I don't tend to keep tabs on my exes, Mary. Sorry."

"What were they like?" I knew how Dark's daughter acted since she wasn't very similar to her dad that meant she had to be like the mother!

Dark's daughter, whose name was Polly, had been a young teen who looked similar to her dad but acted more sweet and cautious, not showing any of his manipulative and talkative characteristics. Before she had died she'd been somewhat of a hero and had turned against Dark on numerous occasions before her death.

Her death had been what pushed him completely over the edge so even if I did mess up and the wife died, I would still know how to prevent Polly's death. That wouldn't be for years, though, since Dark was still single and childless...unless it was an accidental pregnancy.

Gah. I had spent so many years pouring over the books and still didn't know anything!

"What were they like? Um..." Odette looked up at the ceiling, scrunching her nose in deep thought. "They were pretty...Um...T hat's all I know. Sorry. It's hard to tell how someone acts when you don't know them personally."

I sighed, knowing this wouldn't get me anywhere. The only options I had right now would be to either ask Derek himself, which wouldn't happen, or just keep by his side until the potential bride appeared.

"But," Odette continued, leading me around the bar and pointing me toward the customers. "Since he just walked in, you can ask him yourself."

"What?"

As my boss shoved me toward the front of the bar my eyes desperately scanned the faces of everyone nearby and finally landed on the familiar dark hair and mischievous eyes of Derek. He was seated at a far table with what I guessed were his friends.

I knew I had to do my job and take their orders but, for some reason, it felt embarrassing to be seen working at a bar with all this makeup on. It might look like I was insecure and trying to cover up my face, which wasn't the case. Not that wearing makeup equaled insecurity but...I didn't know. I was just making up excuses not to talk to the villain of the story.

As I walked toward Derek and his obnoxiously loud friends, I found myself focusing every ounce of attention on my legs as they moved. Unfortunately, I think paying attention to my steps was making my movement even less graceful.

"See? I told you she was pretty," I heard one of the guys whisper in Derek's direction. He was trying to lower his voice but had likely already started drinking because he wasn't doing a good job of it.

"Can I get you anything?" I started to ask but froze as soon as Derek looked my way with a bored expression on his face. Our eyes locked for a moment and I felt my heart skip a beat, then he looked away as though nothing had happened and ordered one of the strongest drinks we had available.

As I wrote down the other boys' orders my mind raced with questions about his actions. Was he ignoring me to hide our "relationship"? Did he not recognize me? Or did he just not care?

The breath I'd been holding in the whole time was finally released when I turned on my heels and strutted away, numbly handing Odette the list of orders as I got over the nervousness and returned to normal. I didn't even know why I was feeling so nervous.

"That's interesting," Odette whispered as she studied the paper and started throwing together the drinks, letting me rest and lean against the edge of the counter to give my limp legs a break.

"What is?" I asked.

The woman shot Derek an odd look, then frowned. "I've known plenty of men in my time," she began, resting a dark green bottle on the tray to be taken out. "And the way he looks at you..."

I waited, confused as to what she was getting at.

"....It's not with the eyes of a man."

"Huh?" Not with the eyes of a man? What did that mean? And why was she giving me another look of pity? "What are you talking about?"

"I'm saying you should break up with him, hun. He doesn't see you as a woman."

"Then what does he see me as?"

Her eyes went wide as she whispered the dreaded words. "A waitress."

No!

Chapter 8

It was starting to get dark by the time I reached the house, my makeup removed and uniform replaced with some purple pants and a black sweater I'd found cheap in a nearby store. Odette had loaned me the money to buy it since my whole paycheck was going to Derek and his grandma.

My mind was still reeling about Dark's lack of reaction to my job but everything became focused when I heard a resounding crash from behind the front door. Panicking, I unlocked the door with the spare key I'd been given and ran inside, listing all the things that could be happening in my head.

The scene I found inside made me want to curl up in a ball and hide.

Derek was pressed against the wall, the right side of his head covered in blood, and his grandmother was at the other end of the kitchen with a long glass shard in her hand.

Lying next to Derek were the remains of a glass pot, which had presumably broken when it hit his head. That meant grandmother had been the one to throw it.

I was in too much shock to clearly hear what the old woman was yelling about but her voice was so full of venom that I didn't need to know. Panicking, I ran toward Derek and wrapped my arms around his head to protect him from any future blows.

Normally, I would have tried to save my own skin in this situation but since I knew how important this moment was I knew that I had to act! I'd seen this exact scene occur in the book and knew how it would end. I hadn't been expecting it to happen so soon but this was the day when Derek's grandmother went too far and tried to kill him for no reason at all. This was the day that Derek made his first kill. It was his first step toward becoming Dark.

I couldn't let that happen!

"It's okay, Dark," I whispered to him as though speaking to a child. In the heat of the moment I'd forgotten to call him by his real name. "It's fine. I'm here."

"Get away!" Grandma yelled, calling me some unsavory names before grabbing my elbow and trying to yank me off her grandson. Luckily, she wasn't quite as strong as me and I managed to maintain my grip.

"Get off of me. You'll get hurt," Derek whispered, looking genuinely concerned about me before shoving me to the side and grabbing both of his grandmother's hands.

All I did was watch as he squeezed her wrists so tight that the shard of glass fell to the floor with a clink and she started to scream as though he had been the one to attack her. I had to cover my ears to keep them from ringing in response.

It was then, as the old woman flailed around helplessly and kept yelling death threats to his face that Derek frowned, looked down his nose at her, and growled like some sort of beast. "I'm sick of tolerating you," he hissed, releasing one of her wrists and wrapping his free hand around her throat. "Why don't you just die?"

Oh no! This was worse than the actual scene had been! Had my interference made it even worse?

Not needing to second guess myself, I leapt to my feet and grabbed the arm used to strangle her, my voice turning even and calm.

"Please," I whispered so he'd focus those dark, angry eyes toward me instead of her. "Don't do this. It'll only drag you down to her level."

"And you think I care about that?" he asked me, turning back to concentrate on the task at hand. His words were less angry when directed at me but it still wasn't enough to stop him.

"Please...Derek...I know that you're a good person. You're not thinking straight right now. Later, once you've calmed down, you'll regret doing this." Now I was just saying whatever came to mind. "If you do this you'll—"

"Yes, listen to her," the woman said, her words reminiscent of a witch and her eyes of a clown. She didn't care if she died. She just wanted to see her grandson end up as miserable as she was.

As soon as she spoke, Derek tightened his grip, squeezing so hard that I could see the veins pop out on his neck.

"Derek!" I yelled, tugging harder on his arms this time. "If you do this, you'll be doing what she wants!"

Only that made him hesitate and glance my way, his eyes seeming to grow lighter with realization. I knew that I had him now and just needed to keep going.

"You're so close to getting that job at Hikarius! Don't let a murder ruin your clean slate and take away your chance to get hired!" I knew that he'd get the job either way but he didn't need to know that. "You still have a chance to become the hero you've always dreamed of."

To show that I trusted him, I removed my hands and took a step back, leaving the decision up to him. I didn't care if he killed the evil woman but I did care about him getting blood on his hands.

The second kill is apparently always easier so, if he didn't kill her now, that meant he would hesitate when the next chance to kill someone arose.

...Goodness, I was talking about murder as if it was the most normal thing in the world.

Derek glanced at me one more time, his eyes clear and face now devoid of expression, then nodded. "Fine." Dragging his only living relative across the floor, he opened the door and flung her onto the street. "If you ever come back," he told her as she sat up, moaning, "I'll kill you."

With that, he slammed the door behind her, locked it securely, and turned toward me with a huge smile on his face. "We'll have to get a better lock," he told me cheerfully, touching the deep cut on his face as though this was the first time he'd noticed it. "Maybe I should get a dog too. I could teach him to recognize her scent."

It was then, when Derek was smiling and the horror was over, that I allowed myself to collapse on the floor and take a deep breath. I had done it. I had stopped him from killing his grandmother. I had changed the future.

Derek was still in the midst of smiling when he noticed my position and got down beside me, checking to see if I'd gotten hurt. When it became obvious that I wasn't cut or bruised he asked me, just to make sure. "Are you okay?"

"I'm fine," I eeked out, unable to take my eyes off the cut on his forehead. "You should probably bandage that."

"You're right." He nodded and got to his feet but before he could head to the bathroom he paused and took a huge breath, sighing. "I haven't felt this good in ages."

Hearing that made me want to giggle like a fangirl. This was the first time I'd gotten the chance to see my idol smile instead of smirk. "Does that mean you won't kick me out?" I hated to ask but was too impatient not to.

Oh. There was the smirk I was talking about. "We'll see," he said, offering me a hand so I could get up. "We'll see."

Chapter 9

My ears twitched when a third scream rang through the halls, dragging me away from the sleep I'd been so close to reaching. Moaning in exasperation, I dragged myself out of bed and turned on the light, squinting my eyes so they couldn't get burned by the brightness.

What was the point of giving her my grandmother's room if she still insisted on keeping me up all night with her screaming? If she hadn't kept me from committing a crime I definitely would have kicked her out alongside my stupid grandma.

Stomping out of my bedroom and toward her new one, I slammed the door open as loudly as I could. "Mary!"

She was writhing around in the small bed, her blankets strewn about and one of her pillows lying dejectedly on the floor. From the movement of her arms it would appear she was attacking someone or being attacked in her sleep. And earlier she'd been bragging that she never had nightmares.

"Mary!" I yelled again only to be outdone by her own cries. Feeling heat rise up in my throat, I grumbled in annoyance and picked her up like a princess, carrying her now motionless body to my room.

"A dog would be quieter than you," I informed her sleeping self as I laid her back down on my bed and crawled in next to her, ready to exchange some well rested sleep for hand holding.

"Maybe I should hire a doctor," I muttered to myself as sleep started to crawl back. "Or invest in some ear plugs," I added, my words beginning to slur before fading out.

Then, she yelled again.

Jerking upright and bonking my head on the top bunk, I hissed and intentionally fell off the bed so I could moan on the floor for a minute or two. It was bad enough to have a giant cut on my head and now this? Was there no end to my misery?

"Dark, don't!" she continued to yell, once again moving around restlessly.

Who was Dark, anyway? I'd heard her call me that when we were fighting Grandma and had ignored it at the time. Was Dark some other person she used to know or was she just really bad at pronouncing my name?

"Don't! I love you!"

My head shot up. "What?!?"

"So uh..." I tried to keep my voice calm as I ran my knife over the pancakes she'd prepared for breakfast. "What did you dream about last night?"

Mary's eyes went wide and she leaned across the table with a sympathetic look in her eyes. "Was I screaming again last night?"

"Just tell me what you dreamed about!" I yelled, slamming my fist on the table and causing her to lean away again, her eyes wide. I paused. "Sorry. I'm just...tired... Sorry."

"It's fine," she managed to whisper cautiously before taking another bite. "At first I was dreaming about what happened with your grandmother." She gestured to the spot on the floor where they'd fought. "Then I started dreaming about my parents." Her eyes grew watery at that and she looked away.

"Oh." Thank goodness! She was just saying "I love you" to her dead parents. What a relief! Not a relief that her parents were dead, of course, but a relief that she wasn't saying it to me.

Okay. Time to change the subject. "Where do you work?" I didn't really care but it was the only question I could come up with in the heat of the moment.

Strangely, she seemed to give me a 'you don't know?' look before shrugging. "At a restaurant, I suppose."

"You suppose?"

"Well, yeah. We serve drinks and food so..."

"Is it a bar?"

"...Yes."

"Okay, fine." I looked away, wondering why she was so hesitant about telling me. It's not like I'd go to every bar in town in the hopes of finding out where he worked. I was just attempting to make conversation. "Make sure to keep an eye out for my grandmother in case she comes back."

"I will. I think I'll buy some sort of self-defense weapon when I find the time."

"Okay, good." All right. That was enough talk for me.

Rising, I pulled on my black jacket and started toward the door, ready to take some more tests and bring myself closer to a job at Hikarius. I was about to step outside when Mary spoke up on more time.

"Have a good day at school!"

"What are you, my wife?" I asked mockingly, casting her a sideways glance before exiting the building as quickly as I could.

Strange. It was supposed to be cold out today but it seemed unusually hot, especially around my face and chest. Maybe I wouldn't be needing my jacket after all.

Chapter 10

I never really cared about Odette.

In the books she was just a pretty face with very little character development. She supported the main characters but never took part in the action and was just, to be perfectly honest, downright boring and predictable. Granted, I was still excited to see her because she was a familiar face. I was desperate for anything familiar in this world.

So, it came as somewhat of a shock to me that she was the person I talked to most in Manica, partly because none of the other characters had shown up yet. I had especially been looking forward to seeing Jala and Maddox, two of the most prominent heroes, but based on the timeline they could still be kids right now. Ugh. I was going to be an old woman by the time anything exciting happened.

Instead of gun fights and mysteries, I was stuck behind a bar telling Odette about my non-existent love life with Derek in the hopes that I'd get some information out of her, which I never did.

"He didn't recognize you?" Odette scoffed at his foolishness before pausing to hand one of the robots a customer's drink. "Are you going to tell him?"

"Of course. I don't want to—"

"Don't!" she suddenly interrupted and grabbed both of my hands in desperation. "Please don't tell him! It'll be so funny to see him talk to you and not realize who you are."

This time I was the one to scoff. "You want me to lie to him?"

"No, just don't tell him. Oh! And if he asks your name just make one up like...." She paused to think, her eyes shining from joy. "Ooh! I know! Call yourself Jacelyn! It's pretty."

"Jacelyn?" It did sound like a nice name but..."No." I shook my head and grabbed a nearby bottle to wash it. "If he asks, I'll tell him the truth....maybe." Unless I froze up like an idiot for some reason, then maybe I'll do it.

"And if he doesn't?"

"Then he'll never find out."

"Excellent."

Growing fed up, I glared at her to show my annoyance. Unfortunately, it only served to make her laugh and trot off to serve more of her customers. As I watched her leave I dramatically rolled my eyes. She was a piece of work. I wasn't even sure if she was a good person or not. She'd seemed so mature in the books.

"Back to work," I muttered, forcing myself to actually wash dishes since I had rent to pay. As I worked, I started humming the Manica theme song, pleased at the irony it created. I was moving onto the third verse when Odette suddenly walked past, nudging me but not saying anything.

Surprised, I looked up from my work to see what was wrong and spotted Derek entering through the front door with two of his friends. Realizing why Odette had poked me, I smiled.

"Aren't you going to serve them?" I asked her sweetly, acting as innocent as physically possible.

"I'm the boss. I'm supposed to just sit back and nitpick everything you do." To prove her point, the woman plopped down in one of the chairs and waved for me to get moving. The joke was on her, though, because as she waved, one of the serving robots zipped past and, thinking she was motioning for him to do it, served the group of boys.

"Ha!" I yelled at her, grinning cheekily.

"What do you think she is?" one of my friends asked. He had been talking about that blonde waitress ever since we'd come in and it was starting to get annoying. "An eight? Seven?"

"I think she's a person, not a number," my best friend, Ace, said as he accepted the drink held out by one of the robots. Ace was as kind hearted and logical as one could get and his straight, blond hair and brown jacket reflected that.

"You're boring, Ace. Derek, what do you think?"

"I think you should buy me a drink," I answered nonchalantly, holding back a laugh when he got red in the face.

"I'm serious, guys. I want your opinion before I ask her out."

"Why don't you..." Ace leaned forward. "Get to know her before you ask her on a date?" He said it like it was the most unique idea ever known to man.

"Or just ask her out and get it over with," I suggested, not caring either way. "You'll break up with her in two weeks anyway so it doesn't matter what we think."

The boy whimpered, then froze, his eyes gradually growing wide and threatening to pop out of their sockets. "She's coming this way," he hissed, trying to adjust his position so he'd look cooler. "You have to help me."

Ace didn't answer but I laughed in his face. "Not a chance."

"Excuse me." The pretty girl in question stopped before our table with an empty tray in her hands, her eyes almost as wide as my love struck friend's.

Now that I'd given her a once over I had to admit that she was good looking but couldn't compare to my last ex in the beauty department. Plus, since my last relationship I'd decided to base everything on personality so I wouldn't get dumped or cheated on again.

Man, she was wearing a lot of makeup, too. She'd probably look like a completely different person under it all. Not that I really care d....She kind of looked similar to Mary, in a weird, overdone kind of way. I don't think Mary would ever consider having a job like this, though. She seemed too innocent to serve drunk men all night.

The girl glanced my way, then nervously pulled a lock of hair behind her ear and turned to my level-headed friend.

"Sorry if this is random but...Are you Ace?"

He nodded, acting surprised. "Yes, I am. Do I know you?"

"I'm a big fan," she gushed, lowering the tray she'd been clutching against her chest and shaking his hand. "My name's Jacelyn and I've been...I heard about you from an acquaintance of mine. They said that you were the best sharp shooter in their class."

"I'm not sure if that's true but...Who did you hear it from?"

"Oh, I..."

At that point I blocked out her voice and turned toward my other friend. His face was downcast and as soon as he caught me staring he focused his gaze on the floor, pouting.

"Better luck next time," I whispered, patting him on the leg until he swatted my hand away.

Oh my goodness. Oh my goodness. Oh my goodness.

I just got to meet Ace. The Ace. One of the main heroes of Manica! The sidekick of Jala, the sharpshooter of the group, the possible love interest of Jala, the...

Wow. It was like meeting three different celebrities in two weeks.

I was so glad I had come!

Chapter 11

The shrill beeping of Dark's alarm clock was what woke me from my dreamless sleep. Ever since I'd started holding hands with him during the night I'd failed to have any dreams about monsters or my family dying.

Groaning as loudly as I could to let my sleep mate know that he needed to turn off his alarm, I turned toward him and pulled my numb hand out from under his. As I shook it to get the stabbing needles out, I nudged him angrily.

"Derek! Wake up!" When I'd first moved here I never would have had the guts to yell at him like this but now that I'd been away from home for a full month, being around him didn't frighten me anymore. I had adjusted quickly.

Derek opened one eye to look at me then rolled over and tried to go back to sleep. "Leave me alone. I'm sick."

My mind flashed back to what he'd been excitedly telling me about the night before. "No! You have to go to school. The Hikarius exam is today. If you skip it you'll be destroying your only chance to get in."

In response, the stubborn boy started coughing up a storm, making it clear to me how much phlegm really was in his throat. It sounded painful.

Pity ran through my insides but I knew that I couldn't let him fail. Losing his dream could be another event that could sent him over the edge, though in the books he didn't get sick on the exam day.

Biting my tongue, I placed both arms under his back and started to lift him out of bed, taking care not to hit his head on the top of the bunk. "Come on, Derek," I whispered as I climbed out after him, leading him toward the closet. "I'll go there with you. You just need to write it for one hour and then you can go home. It'll be fine."

"I can't," he moaned, slumping over weakly and letting his head rest on my shoulder, something he normally wouldn't do. "I'm so...tire d..."

He seemed fine yesterday so it must have been the nervousness...I wondered if I would get whatever sickness it was because we slept in the same bed.

"Come on." I stood my ground and picked up his favorite blue sweater, pulling it over his pajama top. I then started searching for his boots. There was no way I was changing his pants so he'd have to settle for the black sweat pants he was sporting.

"If you pass, we'll go celebrate at Odette's, okay?" I bribed as he stumbled toward the front door like a child, forgetting that he wasn't wearing any shoes. I couldn't help but laugh as I ran after him and insisted he put the boots on before stepping into the cold.

"I don't think I'll make it," he whispered before I shoved him out the door.

By the time we reached the entrance to his school he was starting to gain more energy but all I could do was hope it was enough to last through the test. Waves of relief flooded through me when I spotted Ace approaching us from the front door.

"Ace will take you in," I told Derek as he stepped away from me and pulled the top of his turtle neck over his mouth to keep out the cold.

As I watched him form a sort of half mask with it, I chuckled. "So that's what that's for," I giggled, pointing toward it and making his eyes squint in annoyance. Frowning, he pulled it down to show his disgust, to which I just laughed again and pulled it back up. "Don't. It looks cute."

As soon as I uttered those words, a small bit of pink started to form on his cheeks. It could have been from the sickness or the cold but...

"Thanks for bringing him here." Ace interrupted our interaction by pulling Derek's arm over his shoulder and helping him stand. "I can get him inside from here and ensure that he stays awake during the test." Ace was applying for Hikarius too, though I don't think he was as obsessed with getting in.

"Thanks," I answered, nodding and looking Derek over one more time to make sure he was okay.

"No problem..."

I froze when I realized that the blond was studying me and my heart dropped when realization dawned in his eyes. He'd recognized me from Odette's.

"Hey, you're..."

My eyes went wide and I desperately whispered "don't" and "no" in his direction.

"...You're the one I passed in the supermarket yesterday," he finished, expertly hiding what he'd originally been saying. It was a good thing Dark was so sick, though, since he might have caught on under normal circumstances. "Well, we'd better get going, eh Derek?"

"Sure," Derek muttered before offering me a tiny wave and heading into the building with me watching like a proud mother. I knew he'd pass. There was no need to worry.

"Congratulations on passing!!!"

I grinned as Ace, Mary, and I clinked our glasses together before I chugged the light alcohol down before they could. Of course, I finished first and got to watch in amusement as Mary struggled to drink the whole thing without stopping.

It was odd. She didn't seem the type to attend these sorts of places but she appeared totally comfortable. Maybe I'd read her wrong.

As soon as she caught me staring I forced myself to look away to avoid any embarrassment. Didn't want her getting any wrong ideas. But, of course, the only other direction to look was toward the bar where my ex was standing, chatting up some customer.

And she saw me. Great. Now she was coming over to say hi. Just what I needed.

"Hey, guys!" The dolled up woman rested her hand on top of my chair and leaned toward Mary with a gleeful expression. "How's everyone doing? Do you need some more drinks?"

"I can buy the next round," Ace offered before digging around in his pockets for change. He never seemed to carry a wallet, probably in an attempt to avoid people asking him for money.

"How are you doing?" Odette finally asked me as I kept my eyes trained on Mary, who was helping my best friend count his coins. Rolling my eyes, I looked her way once to satisfy her, then turned back to my friends again.

"I'm fine," I answered curtly.

"How are you and Mary doing?" she asked, making it clear what she was hinting at.

"Fine." There was no way I was telling my ex about my current non-relationship. But now that I thought about it... "How do you know Mary's name?"

"Hmm?" Odette mockingly batted her eyelashes, pleased that she knew something I didn't. "She's a regular here. I see her almost every day."

"What?" I tried to keep myself from acting outwardly shocked but Odette already knew she'd managed to surprise me. What was Mary doing here every day? And why hadn't I seen her?

The bar tender smiled as she watched me mull over the information but I ignored her. I had more important things to think about.

Was Mary not aware of how dangerous it was here? I took a sip of my second drink while keeping an eye on her from across the table. I knew she could probably handle herself but...I couldn't help but want to make sure she stayed safe. I couldn't have some creep trying to trick or manipulate her.

Maybe I'd stop by the bar tomorrow just to make sure she was okay. After all, if she got hurt there'd be no one to pay my rent, right? Right.

Chapter 12

Here he was again, coming in by himself for the second time. As I watched him take a seat in the darkest available corner, making himself comfortable and training his eyes on the entrance, I couldn't help but admire how good he looked in his black top and pants. The dark fabric showed off his lean build and the v neck left just enough room to see his pronounced collar bones. I hadn't considered him very good looking in the comics but now that I'd been around him for so long his looks were beginning to very gradually grow on me.

Realizing that I was awkwardly staring at him, I forced myself to look back at the drink I was making. His presence shouldn't distract me.

I had just handed the fresh drink to one of Odette's metal assistants when the woman herself sauntered up to me, this time wearing a short, red dress with black tights underneath. Grinning like a child, she leaned her head daintily on my shoulder.

"I told him you're a regular here," she whispered in my ear, making the back of my neck tense up. "He's waiting here to keep an eye on you when you arrive."

A light bulb went off in my head. So that's why he was staring at the front door so intently. Knowing why he was here made my chest warm a little but then it turned icy with guilt when I realized that he was wasting his time.

"I should tell him who I am," I told the woman, shrugging her off and straightening the front of my uniform. "He could be studying or hanging out with friends right now."

There I went again, trying to act like a responsible mother to ignore how much I liked seeing him here. And knowing he came here for me and me alone made me incredibly happy.

...Dang it! I wasn't here to fall in love with Dark. I was here to take care of him. That was it!

"But if you tell him now, it'll spoil the fun," Odette moaned immaturely before smirking and adjusting her skirt. "Why don't you serve him while I take care of those gentlemen over there?" She pointed to her destination before flirtatiously walking away and leaving me to ponder my life decisions.

After giving it some painful thought, I stepped out from behind the counter and a bit too forcefully slammed a drink on his table, making him jump a little and shoot me a look of annoyance.

"It's on the house," I told him, trying to flash a flirtatious smile but failing, too nervous to convince my lips to turn upwards. It didn't matter anyway, though, since he just smirked and nodded his thanks before taking a sip. Receiving free drinks must have been the norm for him.

Sighing inwardly, I decided to mimic Odette and sat down next to him, doing my best to raise one eyebrow so I'd seem more like my boss and less like myself. My main objective was to get a reaction out of Dark but nothing I'd done so far was weirding him out.

I guess it was time to turn things up a notch.

Inwardly giggling at how much freedom I had in this disguise, I rested both hands under my chin and leaned toward him, flashing a toothy smile. "Do you have a girlfriend?"

Derek glanced at me with an expression of amusement I hadn't seen before. "...Sort of. Why do you ask?"

My entire body tensed up and I felt my heart stop beating for a second, which kind of hurt. "What's her name?" This was the first I'd heard of it. Was she the woman he'd marry?

Oh. There was another expression I'd yet to see. This one consisted of his eyes shining a little and the corner of his mouth rising slightly. He looked...really attractive when he smiled like this.

Ugh. What was I now? Some kind of crazy fangirl? Why did I keep thinking about his appearance? So superficial!

"It doesn't matter now." He rubbed the back of his neck and looked out the window at the large moon hanging out among the stars. "I'll be moving into the Hikarius Company in a couple of weeks so we won't be seeing each other again."

"What?" I couldn't keep the shock out of my voice.

"Yeah." He smiled again, awkwardly this time. "We're only allowed to bring our legal family to live with us so..." His voice trailed off as his eyes shifted back and forth, muttering things under his breath to himself.

As I sat there, my mouth hanging slightly open, my mind scrambled to find a plan B. All thoughts about messing with Derek were gone and replaced with panic. He was moving and I couldn't come with him. If he wasn't even going to bring his girlfriend with him then he wouldn't even consider dragging me along. What was I supposed to do? Would I have to get a job there so I could keep an eye on him?

"I suppose I could tell my boss that we're married. I might get away with it but..." He thought some more, then turned toward me, finally remembering that I was still here. "What do you think I should do?"

I was surprised he was asking me, a complete stranger, about his love life. "Um...That doesn't sound like such a bad idea," I blurted, still worried about my own situation. But if he married this woman, it would make it way easier to know where she was and how to protect her from death.

I was way too young to be carrying this much weight on my shoulders. Maybe I really should tell Odette about my situation and get her opinion on it. Would telling the main characters my secret break a forth wall or something?

"Maybe you're right but I don't know if I want to marry someone when I haven't known them for that long." He really was taking my opinion seriously. It was cute.

"Well," I used the most professional voice I could muster, "If it's a fake marriage then you don't need to worry. If things don't work out then you can just break up and no one will be the wiser."

As I watched him nod, I immediately regretted my rushed answer. I didn't agree with ending a relationship just because it wasn't going perfectly. But it's not like we were talking about me so I let it slide.

"Hmm. You're right."

"Really?"

He laughed. "Yeah. Thanks for helping me out." Looking thoroughly satisfied, he leaned back in his seat, a position he took quite often, and started watching the front door again, giving me an opportunity to leave. Now was definitely not the right time to reveal my identity.

As I headed back to my post I happened to glance at the clock and realized that my shift ended in two minutes. Awesome! I could change out of these clothes and...hmm.

I had to take a moment to catch my breath and make sure my outfit didn't look like it had just been thrown on, which it had, before I rounded the corner of Odette's building and entered through the front door, attempting to act as nonchalant as possible.

It was almost closing time so most of the customers were slowly starting to filter out after drinking their fill and the tiny robots were using giant, red cloths to clean off the dirty tables. I didn't think there was anyone left to recognize me, which was exactly what I'd wanted.

As I headed toward the bar where Odette was waiting with a smirk, I intentionally ignored the young man sitting in a corner booth with his eyes trained on me. I could feel his stare burning into my side.

I was almost close enough to call out to my boss when Derek suddenly walked up beside me and grabbed my elbow, causing me to finally look up into his frightening eyes. "Derek? What are you doing here?"

"They're about to close," he informed me before nudging me toward the exit.

"But I just got here," I pleaded as we stepped out into the darkness and I started to feel the cold bite into my arms and cheeks. Derek was still keeping a tight hold on my arm like he thought I was about to run away.

"Why are you out here when it's so dark?" he demanded in a soft but commanding tone. "It's dangerous at night."

I decided to turn his words on himself. "What are you doing out so late?"

"I was..." He turned toward me angrily, then paused before he could put his foot in his mouth. "...Thinking about something important."

"Like what?"

"None of your business."

"Okay." I had to admit this was a little funny but probably not worth all the needles of guilt that kept shooting through my sides. "Do you want to talk about it?"

Recently, he'd been telling me everything about his future job and how much of a jerk his new boss was so why hadn't he told me about his girlfriend? That seemed equally important. Maybe it was just awkward 'cause I was a girl.

Derek seemed to hesitate and almost started to say something, then he caught the gossipy look in my eyes and clammed his mouth shut, frowning. "No. Let's just go home and lock up the house. I don't want to risk Grandma finding you alone in the dark and beating you up."

"Oh." So that's what he was worried about. How sweet. "Thank you, Derek."

As soon as I said it, his grip loosened and he smiled. "No problem ...If you ever want to go to Odette's just make sure I come with you."

"Sure thing." I wouldn't mind that. I'd get to spend more time with him before he left. What would I do when he was gone, though?

Chapter 13

I don't think Derek trusted me that much. He still ended up coming to the bar every day for five days straight, then I'd sneak out the back door and come in through the front so he could escort me home. And he still hadn't =mentioned the fact that he was moving away. Was he just planning to hightail out of here one day while I was working so I wouldn't know where he'd gone?

The only good thing that came out of this week was the amount of interesting, personal conversations I got to have with him in my 'Jacelyn the Waitress' disguise, though most of them didn't yield any useful information about him or the world of Manica.

It wasn't until our sixth walk home together that something important actually happened.

I was staring at the ground, trying to avoid the tiny puddles that would likely streak mud along the bottoms of my shoes, when Derek suddenly stopped walking and pulled me toward him, his eyes shooting back and forth between mine as though he was attempting to read my mind.

I suddenly felt nervous. "What's wrong?" Was he finally going to kick me out?

"Mary...Do you..." He cleared his throat, losing his nerve and stepping away so he could take a deep breath, his chest heaving up and down. "Do you know that I'm moving out?"

"No," I lied.

"Well, I am. Hikarius has small apartments built into their company building and I was invited to move there. It's not too far. Just on the other side of town." He pointed toward the more wealthy area where houses weren't made of rotting wood like ours was.

"I'm only allowed to bring family with me," he continued, growing more confident and lowering his voice as he spoke. "So you'll need to..."

I gripped my hands together so tightly that they started to hurt. He really was kicking me out and replacing me with someone else, someone who wouldn't be able to protect him from the future. What should I do? Should I beg him to let me come with him?

"...You'll need to sign a paper stating that we're married if you want to keep living with me," he finally stated, his nervousness vanishing once he got the words out.

My jaw dropped, my hands fell to my sides, and I laughed, annoyed at how naïve I had been. He'd been talking about me that one time! And I'd been stupid and assumed it was someone else! Wow. How great was that?!?

Derek didn't seem to understand why I was laughing, though. "Why? You don't want to?"

I shook my head. His brows were beginning to furrow, meaning he was insulted by my outburst, so I needed to hurry and extinguish his fears. "Of course I want to keep living with you."

"And you have no problems with a fake marriage?"

He made a good point.

My body started to shiver as I realized what this meant. I knew it was a fake marriage. I knew it was just a document to trick his boss. But...

"Um..." I felt the blood drain from my face. "It won't be official, right?" I asked, laughing nervously to hide how scared I had become in the last two seconds.

If I became his wife that meant that I could be the one to die. Granted, the wife in the story had already given birth to a daughter before dying but I'd already messed up the timeline once so it could easily happen again.

I will admit, I was starting to find myself attracted to Dark. Maybe it was because of my earlier obsession with him or how close we'd been lately but...there was no way I wanted to be his wife.

That daydream I'd had before coming here had been just that: a daydream! I never, in a million years, wanted to marry the guy! I didn't want to end up dead! I didn't like him that much.

"No, it won't be official," he answered, "But if you want we could secretly date officially if that would make it less awkward." I wasn't sure how his face looked right now because it was too dark. That might have helped me know if he was serious or not.

I knew that Derek could sense my nervousness. He probably knew me well enough to catch on to all the signs by now. So, in order to probably muddle my mind and make me confused enough to say yes, he gently gripped both of my shaking hands in his unmoving ones and pulled me closer.

I had barely managed to look up at his face before he leaned forward and kissed me, holding us together for three seconds with his eyes closed (I knew they were closed because I was too shocked to close mine), then I felt him smile and pull away, a self-confident smirk on his face.

"It's settled, then," he said with a light chuckle before entwining his fingers with mine and continuing toward our house, his steps now more graceful and relaxed. My legs, on the other hand, were barely keeping me up.

Was he that desperate to make me continue living with him and paying rent? Why was he messing with me like this?

Derek Hacket, I didn't care how cute you were, I did not want to marry you and die! If dying wasn't part of the equation I might have considered dating you...maybe...but since it was not I refused to marry you! There was no way!

If I hadn't made it my goal to save your life I definitely would have asked Odette to take me in instead, understood?

Chapter 14

It was easy to not think about that kiss as I walked toward our new apartment because Derek had insisted on letting me handle all the luggage while he and Ace went ahead to "scout out" the place. That meant I carried all the weight and he twiddled his thumbs like a child. I don't know what I ever saw in the jerk.

I had to admit, though, that as I walked up the steps of the tall, arched, steel building with its long windows and actually clean sidewalks, excitement started to rise in my chest. Long gone were the days where we'd have to hide in blankets because the thin walls did nothing to stop the cold. Gone was the smell of burnt toast that lingered anytime we attempted to make breakfast.

But not gone was the sharing of a bed. The only difference would be that this one was bigger.

"What do you think?" Derek asked proudly as he held one of the side doors open for me, blatantly ignoring the three heavy suitcases I was attempting to lug behind me. "Feeling impressed yet?"

"By the building, yes," I retorted, grunting as I shoved one of the bags through the doorway. "By you? No."

The jerk just giggled as I stepped into the long, carpeted hallway. A series of numbered doors lined the hall and I immediately started searching for ours: #9. The sooner I got in there the sooner I could drop these stupid bags.

"It's a pity Ace lives on the other side of the building," Derek pouted as he produced one of our three card keys and slid it into the number nine slot. Despite being mad at my "husband", who had officially become my "spouse" yesterday when we signed the papers, I couldn't help but jump up and down in anticipation of our new home.

When Derek noticed my excitement, he smiled and threw the door open for me, then he grabbed the heaviest suitcase and carried it inside.

"Oh. So now that I've carried it all the way here, you decide to be a gentleman," I muttered playfully before running inside with a childish screech of joy.

It was a little bit smaller than our previous establishment and, other than the bathroom, didn't have any doors to separate the rooms but it was clean and fresh and that was all that mattered to me.

The front door led straight into the quaint kitchen, its counters a coral pink and the pearl walls covered with hanging stainless steel pans. The stove actually looked usable unlike our old, rusty stove, which had looked ready to collapse if we put anything on top of it. There was also no scent of burning food. My nose felt so thankful.

Our only bedroom was off to the left of the kitchen and consisted of a queen sized bed with sky blue covers, dressers on both sides of the bed, and a small window overlooking an empty field of grass. I would get to be woken up by the sun rising instead of waking in pitch blackness.

"I love it," I told Derek as I ran through the apartment to make sure there was nothing else I'd missed. Other than the bathroom, which was white and plain, and a tiny closet for hanging our clothes, there was nothing else to discover but I didn't care.

The villain started to smile again but looked away before I could see it, yawning to make it seem like nothing had happened. "Let's start unpacking," he told me seriously, thinking he could fool me. He couldn't. I knew he was just as thrilled about this as I was.

"Derek is having a nap," I sang to myself as I crept down the halls, the key to his new office clutched in my hand. "So I'm gonna steal his...trap...That doesn't make sense." I shrugged. Oh well. It was a good thing making rhymes was not my job.

Derek hadn't told me how to get to his office but since I'd caught a glimpse of it in the show, I knew exactly where to go. Luckily for me, work hours were over so very few people were around to spot me sneaking about.

It took twenty minutes of wandering the halls and looking for something familiar but I finally managed to discover his new workspace and easily let myself in, a cheeky smirk on my face. I'd get to see it before he did.

The office was tiny, barely the size of our bedroom, but that didn't make it any less interesting. A wall of glass ran between the main desk and the door, which seemed a bit odd, and there was a small bathroom off to the right. If only all offices came with miniature bathrooms.

Since there was nothing else to look at other than the desk, which didn't even have any drawers, I sat down on the rolling chair and scooched forward so I could have a look at the huge, clear computer screen. As soon as I reached out to touch it, the screen turned on and started to hum softly.

My heart was starting to beat wildly with excitement when a purple face made of words and numbers appeared on the screen, making me slide back against the wall in surprise. I hadn't been expecting someone to be in there.

"You must be Derek Hacket's wife," the face said in a soothing but somewhat robotic voice, her purple eyes scanning my face to memorize it. "What is your full name?"

I hesitated, trying to recall seeing a female computer in the series but not remembering anything. Maybe she'd been in the books but hadn't played a major roll. "I'm Mary. And what's your name?"

The computer hesitated, as though unsure how to answer. "My creator called me DIHAN," she answered. As she said the letters one at a time, long strands of hair began to protrude from the back of her head and swirl around her face, giving the impression that she was underwater. "But I'm sure my new owner will give me a new name."

"Derek?"

"Yes. Each new Hikarius employee is given their own personal AI to monitor and assist in their work."

"Hmm." I started to smile. She was interesting and it was a pity I couldn't remember her from the show. "Do you like the name Dihan? I could call you Di instead. It's a bit easier to remember." I pronounced the name Dee and thought it sounded somewhat pretty.

The AI paused, calculated, then nodded. "Very well. Di is satisfactory. But if Mr. Hacket does not approve then I shall change it."

"I'll tell him your name so he can't," I offered, though it was more of a statement than a suggestion. Moving closer to her again, I found myself growing more comfortable. "Are you a self-aware AI?"

"I have been programmed to give the appearance of self-awareness and adjustment but do not feel human emotions. I can pretend to if you wish."

"That's okay. I'm not a fan of pretending." I smiled, then suddenly felt a lightbulb go off in my head. "Wait! Di, are you good with technology?"

The AI calculated again, then frowned. "I do not underst—"

"See," I reached down into one of my back pockets and, as though holding my most prized possession, showed her the dead phone I'd brought with me. "I have this phone and it's not working for some reason. It's got some …files on it that I need to see. Do you think you'll be able to fix it?"

She examined the device in confusion, likely not recognizing its make or model, then shook her head. "I cannot fix it but may be able to extract the information for you."

"Really?" I'm sure she was just simplifying her words to make it easier to for me to understand. "That'd be great. It's got some really important stuff on here that I can't afford to lose." Super important! Like, future telling important.

"If you insert it in here..." A compartment in the nearby wall opened, allowing just enough space for me to slip the useless phone inside. "...Then I'll see what I can do."

"Awesome!" I turned to leave, sure that Derek was close to waking up by now. Before I could exit, though, I remembered something and stopped. "Oh! And Di?"

"Yes, Mary?"

"Don't tell Derek about anything you find on there, okay?"

"Very well."

"Thanks!" I waved and ran off, allowing the door to shut behind me. This day just kept getting better and better.

Chapter 15

Today was going to be a good day. I could feel it.

As Ace and I walked down the halls toward my "husband's" office, I felt the tips of my fingers tingle and the hair on the back of my neck stand on end. Once I got Derek out of his office I'd be able to see what was on that phone and review everything I needed to know about Dark and Manica. It felt like years since I'd last had a look at the comics or show.

"So, are you still working at Odette's?" Ace asked, dressed in the black and white Hikarius uniform and carrying some files under his arm. We'd become good friends over the last few weeks and, now that we lived in the same building, it was even easier to run into him.

"Yes but she gave me the week off to 'adjust'." I added quotation marks to the word because she had no idea how much adjustment I'd done when I first came here from another world. Moving into a new house was child's play compared to that.

"Have you told him?" Ace nodded at Derek's office. "I'd assume so since you're married now."

I shot the blond a look of friendly disbelief. "You really don't think we're married, do you?" I asked, laughing. I mean, how ridiculous would that be? Marrying the villain of Manica!

Ace didn't seem to share my amusement. "I think you should tell him," he said, continuing down the hall without me. "He likes you a lot."

"Eventually," I called back as quietly as I could.

Ace was a nice guy, I'd give him that, but he was really reading too much into Derek's actions. Yes, he was his best friend but I'd been watching Dark for years and knew how to read him. Derek didn't like me. He just wanted to take advantage of me like any villain would.

...I just really didn't want it to be true and was making up excuses. I didn't want to become the wife who died and barely got mentioned in the backstory.

I was about to enter Derek's office and say hi when I heard raised voices inside and pressed my ear against the cold door to listen in. What was going on in there?

"You're not getting paid to think, Hacket, you're here to do what I tell you! Now if that's not clear then you and your little wife can pack your bags and go back to whatever dump you crawled out of. Is that understood?"

Oh no. Derek's boss.

"Yes sir."

"Good."

I'd barely managed to back up and stand at attention with my hands behind my back before the scary man, Mr. John Philips, stepped out and bored holes into me with his eyes.

I looked him over meekly. His greying hair and long, grey coat only served to make him look like more of a snobby jerk and the tiny glasses balanced on his nose were so small that I doubt they served any purpose other than to give the appearance of "intelligence".

"Mrs. Hacket." He nodded curtly in my direction before stomping away, unaware that I'd overheard his conversation.

Breathing a sigh of relief, I slipped into the office and locked the door behind me just in case he decided to come back. "What a creep," I muttered, turning to see how Derek was doing. He was leaning against the desk, his hands balled into fists and teeth grinding.

As I watched him stare at nothing, doing his best to hold in his anger, I felt that same sense of pity I'd always had when reading his origin story. Hearing him get yelled at for no reason was just a taste of the cruelties he'd had to tolerate before snapping. The authors had thrown every horrid character they'd ever created into his path just to ensure he became the villain.

As I stood there watching him fight himself I decided that, just for now, I should act as his wife.

Stepping forward, I wrapped both of my arms around his tense shoulders and wracked my brain for encouraging words to say. Of course, nothing came to mind but even touching him seemed to calm him down a bit. I felt his tightened muscles loosen and he leaned forward a little more, his breathing slowing down over time.

"Thanks," he whispered, grasping one of my hands gingerly and continuing to stare at the wall. "...He really is a creep." He chuckled, then sucked in a large gulp of air to keep himself from crying. "Wish Ace and I could have gotten the same boss."

"Yeah." I agreed. Ace's boss was the most chill out of the three Hikarius managers. Derek just happened to get the worst one. "Will you be okay?"

"Yeah. I'm fine." He took one more breath, this time doing it over-dramatically to get a laugh out of me, then pulled away. "Have you met Di? She's my new AI and..." He pulled me closer so he could whisper in my ear. "...I think she's self-aware."

I nodded. "I think so too."

"I'll keep an eye on her," he added jokingly before turning the computer on and allowing her violet face to appear.

"Hello again, Mary," Di began in her calm, monotone voice. "It is good to see you. I have prepared the—"

"That's awesome!" I yelled suddenly, grabbing Derek's hand and pulling him away from the computer while shooting daggers at her coded face. I thought she'd promised not to say anything in front of Derek!

"—The clothes that you ordered yesterday," Di finished without skipping a beat, intentionally staring into my eyes as though saying I could trust her. "They will be waiting in your apartment."

"Oh. Thank you, Di." I bowed politely and released the confused Derek's arm before smiling and pulling a strand of hair behind my ear nervously. Did he suspect something?

He was peering at me with squinted eyes. Yup. He saw right through me.

"Hey, Mary," he started quietly, waving Di away so she'd turn off and give us some privacy. "I want to ask you something. I've been holding back but...this seems as good a time as ever."

My hands turned clammy. Oh no. I wasn't ready to reveal anything yet.

"I want to talk about the day we first met."

"What about it?"

He clicked his tongue. "... I know what you are, Mary."

Chapter 16

How could he know what I was? Who looked at someone and said, "Hmm. That person suddenly appeared in the middle of a field. They must be from another reality that is more real than this one and my world is just a fictional comic book created by someone else"? No one did. He must have been bluffing.

Crossing my arms, I stood my ground. "What am I, then?"

"Don't give me that look," he muttered before continuing. "You're a Valdis."

"What?" A part of my mind exploded at that observation.

The Valdis were people who, for reasons never explained in the books, were born with mysterious powers. They mainly tended to be female, though males were apparently not unheard of, and usually discovered their powers during their teenage years. These powers ranged from teleportation, moving things with their mind, creating weapons out of thin air, and flying.

I had only heard about two Valdis in my history of reading. The first had been a middle aged woman named Ebony who appeared for two chapters before disappearing and never being heard from again. The other was Dark's daughter, Polly. Her powers were part of the reason she died.

But me being a Valdis? "No way," I scoffed. "I think I'd know if I was a Valdis."

He raised an eyebrow. "Have you even bothered to check?"

"Of course!" Everyone checked to see if they had super powers every once in a while, right? Right? ...Everyone except me. Not recently, anyway.

Wait. What if he was actually right? I needed to test this.

"Derek, why don't you go home and have a nap?" I asked, nearly shoving him out the door so I could talk to Di and check to see if I had powers. "I need to use your office for a while."

"But I thought we were going to Odette's," Derek asked, gripping both sides of the doorway so I couldn't force him out completely. "It was going to be our first date."

"We can go later," I answered, not really caring about seeing my workplace right now. Couldn't he see that I had more important things to do? "I'll see you in an hour, okay?"

He still refused to budge. "But we need—"

"Bye." I used as much strength as I could to get him out in the hallway, then shut the door and locked it, not allowing myself to feel bad for him. We could hang out later. Right now I needed answers!

My heart was beating out of my chest again, though this time it wasn't out of anger toward my boss but confusion about Mary. Had I done something wrong? Was I not supposed to know she was a Valdis? Was she mad at me?

I started scratching my head and, not wanting to risk having her hate me, decided to obey for once and walk to my room. I was due for a lunch break anyway.

What was it about Mary that made me rush through so many emotions in so little time? She was so weird and unpredictable that I couldn't help wanting to figure her out, from her dreams to her strange accent to her nervousness when talking about her past.

Plus, she'd destroyed my pride by not mentioning our kiss from earlier. I thought my intentions had been clear but she was still acting like nothing happened. Did she not feel attracted to me at all?

My mind was still abuzz as I walked down the hall, trying to focus on what I should eat instead of why my girlfriend was so mysterious.

I gulped as I stood in the center of the office with nothing but Di to watch me. I felt sweat slide down the side of my face and the palms of both hands start to grow moist. I was so nervous about this.

"If you wish to test his theory, feel free to use it on your phone." Di opened the small compartment in the wall again, causing the phone sitting inside to jump a tiny bit from the movement. "I have extracted everything I can and will show you when you are ready."

"Thanks," I whispered and bit my lip, using one hand to rub the sweat off my forehead and stretching the other toward my phone. I flipped my hand right side up, then upside down to see if it would do anything. Then I focused all my attention on moving the phone with my mind, scrunching my eyebrows together so hard that it send pangs of pain through my forehead.

Nothing but my jagged breaths echoed through the room as we both waited for something to happen. My arm started to ache from the strain and I was about to give up when the tip of the phone slowly started to rise before slipping out of the compartment and crashing to the floor, forming a small crack across the screen.

My heart leapt.

Whirling toward the computer, my jaw dropped. "Did you do that?" I yelled in excitement, pointing at the evidence.

The AI shook her head, her face refusing to betray an emotions. "It would appear that you are a Valdis."

A Valdis. I was a Valdis.

Like mother, like daughter, I guess.

Ugh! Why had I thought that? I was not going to become Polly's mother because I wasn't going to marry Derek!

That reminded me, though. I needed to start reviewing those videos.

"Di." I placed both hands on the desk and leaned toward the screen. "Can you play episode 18. Start twenty minutes in. I want to see the part where Dark...the villain... confesses his past."

"Very well."

In moments, the part of the story that had made me fall in "love" with the villain began to play. I began feeling nostalgic as I watched Dark, looking older and more traumatized than the Derek I knew, stand before the heroes, moments before his breakdown occurred in which he truly morphed into the villain of the story.

"Dark...what's wrong?" Ace asked. "What did Di say?"

Dark turned to him with tears in his eyes. "My wife she...she's dead."

"What? How?"

"I don't know. She..." He paused. "I just talked to her yesterday on the phone. She seemed fine. I don't know why she'd..." He finally started to shake. "She was all I had."

"Well, technically you still have your daughter," Jala started in her typical, sassy tone.

Dark scowled. "You think this is funny?!" he snapped. "What do you know about my wife? She was so delicate and tried so hard to cover up her insecurities with a hard exterior. She was the only woman I ever learned to love and now she's gone forever!"

As he continued to yell, all three of the characters, even Ace who used to be Dark's best friend, started to back away. His eyes were growing dark and the veins were popping out on his arms. They'd never seen him like this before. In the past he'd always been cheery and great at tolerating every issue they'd come across.

"Dark." Ace tried to steady him. "They didn't say anything against your wife. You're just trying to vent your anger—"

"Shut up, Ace!" Dark suddenly yelled, shoving his best friend against the wall.

So they ran, unable to save him from his grief.

On their way out, Jala attempted to kill Dark so he couldn't hurt them but that only made it worse. He saw it as the ultimate betrayal and decided to use his Valdis daughter to control the Hikarius moon station, which he'd planned to use on Manica's citizens.

As I watched the moving scene, I felt my body tense up upon realizing what I'd just done to him moments before. I'd slammed the door in his face. Just like every other person he'd ever met, I had rejected him. I was no better than any of the other characters.

What had I done?

Panicking, I told Di I'd look at the phone later and ran out the door, calling Derek's name and charging toward our room. Hopefully I'd be able to apologize in time.

Chapter 17

When I found my "husband", he was sitting in the kitchen waiting for his food to cook, an opened car magazine in his hands. He had been scanning some of the black vehicles on the second page, I wasn't sure what kind of cars they were since I wasn't well versed in such things, but he dropped it as soon as I entered the room.

"Hey. Back so soon?" He glanced at the square clock on the wall. "It's only been ten minutes."

I paused to catch my breath then sat next to him, so relieved that he wasn't angry at me. "Let's go to Odette's," I gasped, too out of shape to handle running all the way across the building.

Derek laughed, amused by my panting. "You sure you'll be up for it?" he giggled, to which I just squinted my eyes at him. "You didn't seem like you wanted to go...with me," he added quietly, slumping his shoulders and turned to check on whatever he was cooking.

I really had hurt him. He was just trying to cover it up.

He thought I didn't like being around him which definitely wasn't the case. I loved hanging out with Derek. He was fun and interesting. It was just his future I wanted to shy away from. "Of course I want to go. I wouldn't have agreed to it otherwise."

"Really?" Now he wasn't sure if I was taking pity on him.

"Yeah."

"Are you a Valdis?"

I frowned in confusion. "Maybe."

"Did you kill your family?"

My eyes went wide.

To someone from earth this question might have seemed totally out of the blue but to those in Manica it was commonplace when discussing the Valdis. It was common knowledge that the majority of Valdis grew up unaware that they had powers and when they did gain them they'd often lose control and end up harming or even killing the people closest to them. That was why one of the theories about Dark's wife's mysterious death involved Polly killing her accidentally.

After we sat in silence for what felt like seconds but was actually a couple minutes, Derek finally looked away again and apologized, assuming he'd just opened an old scar. "At least now I know how you appeared in front of me so suddenly," he said quietly, more to himself than to me.

If only he knew the real reason. "Do you think we should keep away from each other just in case?" I asked. "I don't want to end up hurting you by accident."

The future villain shook his head. "You're probably at more risk of killing someone without me because of those nightmares."

He was probably right. I wondered how bad it could have gotten during the night if he hadn't been holding my hand. "Okay."

I really was part of this world now. I was one of the mystical Valdis, the most revered beings in Manica.

Maybe my powers had something to do with my arrival here. They might even date back to my days on Earth. Maybe I'd been born with them. Maybe my extreme will to save Derek had created them. I'd probably never know.

...Ugh. One thing was just piling on top of another. Would I be able to handle this much information and stress without breaking down? Maybe I should just stop holding it in and tell Derek who I really was. No, that might risk breaking the fourth wall and sending me back home or something. I didn't know! I didn't know what to do!

My head slammed on the table with a thump and I wrapped both my hands around my head, allowing my fingers to tangle themselves up in my hair. I could feel the beginnings of a headache forming.

"You okay?" Derek was about to reach for me when his timer buzzed and he had to turn off the stove before the food could burn. Once that was complete, he turned back to me, eyes overflowing with concern.

"I'm fine," I whispered, my voice muffled from my position. "I just need a minute." To emphasize this, I moaned loudly out of exasperation.

"Sorry," I muttered miserably, forcing myself to stand. "Just got a lot on my mind. Let's go to Odette's. Going out will do me good."

"Okay. Let's."

I could tell he was trying to hold back his joy at my response, which immediately made me feel guiltier for rejecting him earlier. If he really, truly did like me then I'd have to choose between taking the risk and dating him or shoving him away, a decision that would go against everything I'd been trying to do these past two months. I was more stressed about that than finding out I had super powers.

So, we abandoned the food he'd been cooking in the fridge and headed to Ace's place to invite him to Odette's. As we walked, Derek somehow managed to wrap his fingers around mine and I just couldn't muster enough strength to stop him. I'd save any repercussions from that for my future self.

"Hi, Di." I waved to the computer as I entered the office, still a tad sleepy from going out the night before. As though on a sensor, Di turned on and smiled at me as soon as I spoke up.

Di. Mary had apparently decided to give her that name and it didn't sound all that bad. Made me think of the name Delilah, though, for some reason.

As I sat in my chair and rolled it around the room like a child (it was the one good thing about this office) my eyes centered on a small, black device lying on the floor to my left. After staring at it for a few seconds to make sure it wasn't a bomb or something, I eventually picked it up and studied it's broken, glass cover.

"Di." I held it up to her face. "What is this?"

The AI studied it for a moment, then answered without hesitation. "It is your wife's. She wanted me to extract some files for her."

"Oh?" She could have asked me instead. "What sort of files?"

Di hesitated, something I didn't know it could do, then pulled up a long series of videos on my computer. I quickly placed the device on my desk and stepped forward to have a closer look at these "files".

From what I could see of the colorful screen shots they were cartoons of some kind, which was odd since I'd never seen Mary watch anything in all the time she'd spent with me.

Thrilled that I might actually get to learn something about my girlfriend's past, I reclined in my chair once more and leaned forward eagerly. "Play the first one."

Chapter 18

The first video was labeled "Episode 1" and the rest continued up until "Episode 21: The Final Chapter". Watching these would take a lot of hours from my life. Oh well. I did have work to do but this felt more important since I cared more about Mary than my boss.

"Playing 'Episode 1'," Di stated.

As I watched I had to admit that the art style was really nice to look at. It wasn't completely cartoonish but not realistic either, which was super appealing. Mary had good taste.

The characters were also quite fascinating. They formed a group of three heroes, the most prominent one being an attractive eastern girl with cropped, inky hair. Accompanying her were two men, one who constantly wore some kind of black, robotic suit that blocked his face and the other a blond who looked similar to Ace. I pointed this out to Di but she didn't seem to care.

"I don't think I've seen this show before," I commented, leaning forward so I could get a closer look.

The trio were on some kind of alien planet or moon on a mission to stop the villain, whoever he was. From the loads of gunfire and sarcastic banter involved, I knew I would have fit in well with these guys.

Twenty minutes in the credits were rolling and I was enthralled. I couldn't wait to watch the next episode and was about to press the skip button when a final cut scene appeared at the end of the credits, accompanied by a male narrative mocking the previous actions of the main characters.

The black screen melted into a blood red and cut to a tall, middle aged man with dark hair and a scar across his forehead. I'd assumed he was the one narrating and was therefore the villain based on his tone and posture.

I was about to grin since I'd always liked how fascinating and relatable villains were when the camera zoomed in on his cartoon face and turned black, leaving me to sit in my unstable chair, dumbfounded.

He had my face.

There was no "Oh, he looks kind of similar to me" type thing. He had my face! He had my eyes and my hair that curled a little bit on the ends if it got too long and that scar on his head was the one I'd gotten when Grandma tried to kill me. Now that I thought about it, his voice was almost identical to mine as well although it had become a bit deeper.

"Di..." I whispered, feeling heat rise in my chest again. I clutched the sides of my chair to try to stay calm but it wasn't working. "Di...What was that?"

"It is a show your wife told me not to show you," the computer informed me in her monotone. Obviously, my orders outranked Mary's.

"Mary..." I cleared my throat and pointed at the blank screen. "Mary told you not to show me this?"

"Yes."

I laughed in disbelief. She'd had something like this, a show with me in it, as the villain no less, and she hadn't told me. What had possessed her to create this?

...No. She couldn't have. This was some high production animation. There was no way she'd created this video in two months by herself without making me suspicious. And she never would have cast me as the villain...would she?

On that note, I paused. What was it she had called me when my grandmother attacked us? Drake? Dark?

"Di, what's the name of the villain in this show?"

"Analyzing...Dark Hacket."

Dark Hacket. Too lazy to bother changing my last name, huh?

So, she and someone else, maybe even a team of people, had for some reason, made a show where I was the villain. Why? Why would she base that character on me? What did that accomplish? And why had she kept this a secret from me?

I had to confront her about this. I had been convinced she was someone I could trust and...and how could she even make something like this? Was it related to her Valdis power? Was...was...

I didn't know what to make of this. My mind couldn't even begin to wrap itself around this concept.

I'd question Mary later. Right now I was going to watch the entire show and I wouldn't stop until I reached "The Final Chapter".

Needless to say, all the affection I'd started to feel toward Mary was gone.

And here I'd been believing that she was the only one who'd never betray me.

The heroes walked into a large, round room with computer screens and wires lining every inch of the walls and ceiling. Each of the cords and wires converged into a small, glass cage in the center of the room and sitting inside the cage was a young girl. Her head had been shaved and all that remained were a few tufts of brown hair.

"So if we want to stop Dark, we have to kill her?" the eastern girl verified, looking to her companions for confirmation.

"She's the one powering his gun," the Ace lookalike answered, referring to the giant weapon Dark had built to exact his vengeance on humanity by destroying all of Manica.

"Fine." The girl rolled her shoulders before pulling out a long sword. "I'll do it."

"Please hurry," the girl inside the box whispered, choking as she spoke. "We don't have much time."

As the armed girl approached, the one inside pressed her hands against the glass. "Please promise me that when you find him, you'll kill him. He is a man who cannot be redeemed."

"Don't worry. I didn't come all the way here just to let him live," the eastern girl answered as she dug her blade through the metal cords. "Why do you hate the guy so much, anyway?"

"Because he's my father."

The blond who looked like Ace walked up to the box and shook his head, pitying her. "Are you sure there's no other way to do this? I don't want you to die."

"I'm more than willing to give my life so long as it kills Dark."

Ace sighed, stepping away. "What kind of a man does this to his own daughter?" he whispered as his friend cut the last wire.

"Mary!!!"

My shout echoed through our tiny apartment, probably disturbing the neighbors next door, but I didn't care. All I cared about was finding my "wife" and asking why she'd lied to my face!

I'd barely managed to make it through Episode 18, which had literally laid out my backstory, but the final episode had been too much. In it, I had died!

"Mary?" I stomped into the bedroom but it and the bathroom were both empty. I was about to start punching walls in frustration when I remembered that she was supposed to go back to work today and stupid me hadn't bothered asking where that was.

"I can't believe this," I cried and collapsed on the edge of the bed, holding my head in my hands in an attempt to stop its ringing.

As I sat there, the ticking of the clock sending shakes through my tensed body, my anger slowly subsided and I felt the sudden urge to cry.

I had been so sure she was the one. She had been kind and loyal and even tried to save me from my witch of a grandmother. She was able to retort my cutting, sarcastic remarks and, even when she got mad, she still managed to keep a level, if dorky, head.

When we signed those marriage documents I had been willing to do it officially. I would have muttered the word "love" if she'd asked me to.

I had never fallen for a girl this quickly and confidently. All of my past relationships resulted in getting dumped or cheated on but Mary had been different from those girls and I'd even started to believe her feelings were becoming mutual.

But this...

I sighed. I needed to clear my head. Maybe some alcohol would do me some good, help me forget. Then I could vent to Odette or that blond girl who always made conversation with me.

Anything would be better than waiting here and crying.

Chapter 19

"And you should have seen episode one!" I told the blond waitress as she filled my cup for the third time. Ever since I'd started talking about this, her eyes had begun to bulge and she'd started listening like her life depended on it. "It was crazy!"

"What happened?" she asked urgently.

"Well," I took a sip and slammed it on the table. "It started with me killing my grandmother, which I totally don't blame myself for since she is a..." I stopped myself from finishing that sentence. "Then...then, I got my job at Hikarius and my boss was just as bad as he is here. And then I got married to some chick that I'd never seen before. Did they even show her onscreen? Anyway, we had a daughter and she looked just like me and I named her Polly and things were great but then..." My voice raised in pitch every time I added a "then".

"Then I got a job working on the moon's space station and I hired these bounty hunters and there were aliens and explosions and things were going great...Then, I got word that my wife died! Imagine that.

And then," another raise in pitch, "the people I was working with tried to kill me for no reason at all. No reason!"

She raised an eyebrow at that as though she assumed I was exaggerating.

"I'm not kidding! After I survived the attack, I was gonna use some alien technology to blow up the world but ..."

This next part made my chest start to burn and I had to clam my mouth shut. Something was clogging my throat. I tried to speak a second time but instead of making noise, tears began streaming down my cheeks and I couldn't stop them.

"Then...they killed my daughter.....Right in front of me. They killed Polly." For some reason, my brain hadn't managed to wrap itself around that thought. "Then when everyone I had ever loved was dead, they looked me in the eyes and shot me in the chest."

Sighing, glad to get that out in the open, I chugged the whole glass and wiped both of my cheeks in hopes of stopping the tears. After seeing her sympathetic face and realizing how I looked, I tried to laugh. "It's kind of funny to get so emotional over a daughter I never even had," I admitted.

"I think it's fine," the girl whispered.

"I just don't understand why my girlfriend would have something like that. Like, how did she even make it?" I laughed again, more forcefully this time. "Can she, like, see the future or something?"

When I looked back up at the waitress I was shocked to see that she too had liquid running down her face. I wasn't sure why. Maybe she was just a really, really sympathetic person.

"Maybe..." She paused and reached a hand out to cover my own, which was an invasion of privacy I didn't appreciate. "Maybe your girlfriend just so happened to be from a parallel universe where you and your world were just a fictional tv show created to entertain teenagers."

I scoffed. "Like that would ever—"

"And maybe," she choked, "she cared about you so much that she came here and met you and decided that she would dedicate her entire life to saving you and your daughter from death."

"That's..." I immediately sobered. "That's...impossible."

The waitress continued to cry but didn't say any more.

As we sat across from each other, both tear stained and full of memories we hadn't asked for, the pieces finally started to fit together.

Mary's sudden appearance in a field. Her avoidance of discussing family. Her clinginess to me. Her nightmares. Her stopping me from killing my grandmother, which had been the first step into my insanity.

And her starting to work for Odette, someone she would have trusted because she was in the show.

"It's not possible," I whispered, my eyes truly opening for the first time. "You can't be..."

Mary nodded. "My world is called Earth and in it, you're just a figment of someone else's imagination. I would have told you but...I thought it might end up destroying the timeline or something." She looked away. "I'm sorry, Derek."

"It's..." I had to turn away too. Starting to feel heat from her touch, I brushed her hand away and rose, the legs of my chair scraping against the floor and grabbing Odette's attention from her spot behind the counter. "I need some time to think about this...away from you."

"I really am sorry, Derek," she repeated, reaching toward me.

"I know you are." I just can't see you right now. "I'll be back later." I turned to leave. "Don't wait up for me."

So I left her there, looking prettier than I'd ever seen her and more stressed than I ever wanted to make her. But she couldn't expect me to just absorb this information and be okay with it. I wasn't as flexible as she was.

Chapter 20

Odette had seen everything so, like the occasionally great boss that she was, she gave me the rest of the night off to wait for Derek's return. She obviously had no idea what was actually wrong but I suppose I'd seemed distressed enough to warrant the break.

Unfortunately, as I sat in the apartment waiting for Dark to return, if he ever would, there was nothing to do but think. Eventually, after growing tired of watching the hands on the clock move and trying to remember if Odette's backstory had ever been given in the show, I decided that practicing using my powers would be the most efficient use of my time.

Now, if I remembered correctly, Valdis were only given one of the four powers available to them, two at most. I already had the telekinesis, obviously, but I wanted to make sure I didn't have anything else.

Slowly rising from the kitchen table, I decided to try the most difficult one first to get it out of the way. Teleportation.

Taking a deep breath and focusing all my attention on the floor a few feet away from me, I slowly edged my foot into the air and closed my eyes, praying that if I did teleport, I wouldn't end up inside a wall.

As soon as my foot hit the ground I whipped my eyes open. It didn't feel like I'd moved at all but, instead of moving one mere foot across the carpet, I had moved to the exact spot I'd been focusing on seconds before.

Teleportation. Check.

Next came creating weapons of light out of thin air. This one had always fascinated me since it was the one power Polly apparently had but never utilized so I really wanted to know what it did.

I used the same level of concentration but this time focused on my hands, envisioning a purple sword materializing in my hands. I tried with all my might and...nothing happened.

Okay. X off weapons of light.

Now, for the final power: flight. I'd saved this one for last since it was the one I was most excited about. Ever since I was a child I'd wanted to be a fairy. All of my imaginary friends had been fairies and we'd played in my parent's backyard for hours without letting up.

Same deal. Concentrate. Visualize.

And....Nothing.

"Seriously?" I yelled as I stared at my feet, which were still firmly planted on the floor. Squeezing my eyes shut, I ran a hand through my long hair and sat on the edge of the bed with a huff. "Look, I appreciate that I can teleport and use the force but...my one dream, just gone?"

Well, to be fair, meeting Derek had been another one of my fulfilled dreams but...why not flying?

As I sat there, my arms crossed and mouth contorted into a childish pout I started to giggle at how silly I was being. I had superpowers and was acting like a baby. How hilarious was that?

"If I want to start controlling my powers I'll have to practice every day," I muttered to myself, planning ahead. "I should definitely make Di find out the whereabouts of Ebony for me." Since she was the only other Valdis I knew and would likely have more experience, I could use my salary to have her teach me. Plus, if and when Polly was born, she could teach her how to control her powers too.

If I ever got to see Polly. At the rate I was going, Derek would probably kick me out.

I was in the midst of lifting a plate in the air with my powers, a task so physically exhausting that I was sweating, when the front door opened.

I had it hanging a couple inches off the table when Derek walked in, his face not nearly as pale as it had been earlier and his hair no longer looking like bedhead. As soon as I spotted him out of the corner of my eye I dropped the plate and it cracked on impact, making me scream a little out of surprise.

The plate didn't matter, though. As soon as it fell I ran toward Derek, nervous and apprehensive about what he'd say.

"Hey, Mary." He slowly shut the door, shooting the broken plate a funny look before gesturing for me to sit down. "Why don't we sit down?"

I immediately slipped into the closest chair and placed both hands on top of the plate as though to hide it. Derek did the same but was a lot slower. It was as though he'd become a computer and was malfunctioning.

It was a relief to see some of the color return to his cheeks. He'd looked like death in the bar earlier and the alcohol hadn't helped. Now he seemed like himself again, which made sitting across from him a tad easier.

"Listen." The future villain gradually reached out to touch my hand and gently wrapped my fingers in between his as though I was the plate, on the verge of breaking. "I've been giving it a lot of thought and I've decided to believe you."

Thank goodness for that.

"And, since I'm going to believe that you really have seen my future and know the best way to prevent my death and my future daught er's..." He paused, likely trying to find the best way to put this. "I've decided that you are the only woman I can ever trust with my life."

I sighed, my tension released. "Thank goodness for that. I was afraid you were going to kick me out."

"What? Why would I kick you out?" He leaned back in the chair, hurt that I'd even consider such a thing.

"Sorry." I shrugged, wishing he could understand that I'd known him as a bloodthirsty villain years before I got to see him act like the caring but sensitive man sitting before me. "I was just scared, that's all."

His dark eyes roamed my face, trying to read me, then he shrugged too. "It's okay. You didn't let me finish what I was going to say, though. I think that we should get married for real."

"What?" How did he come to that conclusion?

"It'll be much easier for you to defend yourself and..." He paused to remember his future daughter's name. "And Polly since you're a Valdis and you know the future. Plus," he scratched the back of his head nervously, "I kind of l...like you so it'd be fine."

Aha! I heard that! He was going to say "love" but chickened out at the last second. Lucky for me because there was no way I was saying it back!

I liked him as a character, yes, and ... as a man, I suppose. But I couldn't become...

As I tried to make excuses against marrying the guy that I was comfortable with and attracted to, my mind started picturing what it would be like to actually marry him and become Polly's mother. The images it conjured up made his preposition sound really, really tempting.

Ugh! Why was my face heating up?

Derek started chuckling when he saw me start to blush. "Don't worry. I won't rush it. I'm just letting you know ahead of time so it doesn't come as a shock later."

As I sat there, listening to the angel and devil argue in my brain, he leaned forward and clasped my hands in both of his. "You're the only person I want by my side," he whispered, his eyes reflecting mine. "I know you're the only one who won't betray me."

"Is that the only reason you're proposing?" I asked. I said it in a joking tone but was completely serious.

My heart started beating wildly when he laughed again, leaning away to give my face a chance to cool down. "No. I would never propose just because I knew you wouldn't try to hurt me. I'd never ask a girl to spend the rest of her life with me unless I was absolutely, without a doubt, sure about it."

"We've only known each other for two months," I whispered.

"Well, technically you've know me for...how many years have you been watching that show?"

The blush that had started its retreat returned in full force. "Well. ..I've been reading the comic books for four years and the show came out a year ago so..."

"See? Nothing to worry about."

"But you're forgetting that the you I saw was a raging psychopath, right?"

"If you managed to love me when I was acting like that then the me now should be a breeze, right?"

He had a point.

"Fine. I'll...consider it." It would take a lot of begging to convince me to marry him but, as much as I hated to admit it, he already had his foot in the door. "But don't get your hopes up."

The villain's face lit up and I got to watch as his slouched back and frozen arms loosened, making him morph into a monster of confidence and sass. "So, I've been thinking about baby names and was wondering, what do you think of the name Polly?" he asked, a smirk starting to emerge.

"Hideous. I'd never use it in a million years."

"I was thinking the exact same thing."

Chapter 21

1 4 Years Later

A pop song I'd never heard before blared in the front of the military ship, probably in a failed attempt to block out the loud engine. The beat was a little mournful but also full of excitement and it helped get me pumped up for the adventure I'd spent years anticipating.

Pulling my long, blonde hair into a ponytail and securing it with a black hair tie, I took one look at my completely black outfit to make sure nothing was amiss, then I shifted my focus toward the three other people in the ship.

Directly across from me, with her tight panted legs crossed, was a young, Asian woman with a jagged, black bob. Her eyes were slanted and she kept looking me over with her heavily shadowed eyes. It almost hurt to look at her because she was so pretty.

I knew, from years of experience, that she was the main character in our future mission. Her name was Jala and, if her thin but toned body and pretty face didn't give it away, she was the heroine.

Sitting on my side of the ship was a man of unknown age or origin. His body was covered from head in toe in black as night armor made of leather or some other thick material. His face was hidden by a shiny helmet with a sharp, silver V running down the top. I'd only heard him speak once during this whole trip and his voice had been deep and mechanical.

This machine-like man was named Maddox. He was the strong, silent type and one of the most popular characters in the show.

And, finally, there was the person seated next to Jala, a woman whose face I couldn't place. She had straight, black hair that ran to her elbows and blue eyes that could have lit up a dark room. She wore a hood, which she occasionally pulled over her head to mask her expressions and, aside from her flashy high heels, there wasn't anything else that really struck me as memorable.

I wasn't sure why I couldn't remember her name. Maybe she was only here in reaction to something I'd done over these past ten years.

The pilot driving this heavily armored, space-faring vehicle struck me as slightly annoying and childish so I pushed him out of my mind. His off tune singing was slightly amusing, though, I had to admit.

"I do wish he'd stop," the unnamed woman commented loudly, raising her voice so she'd be heard over the songs. Her voice reminded me of Odette's, smooth and controlled with a slight touch of flirtation. She also had an accent that sounded almost British but with a Manica flair.

"I know how to drive a ship," Jala offered quietly, pulling a small knife out of her jacket with an evil gleam in her eye.

"Kill him and we can kiss our paychecks goodbye," Maddox interrupted, crossing his arms and looking out the window at the passing stars.

The dark haired women glanced at each other, then shrugged, deciding they cared more about greed than their bleeding ears.

"So." I leaned forward, trying to keep my voice level. "Is this your first time to the moon?" I wanted to ask what the third girl's name was but it might seem weird since I already knew what the other two's were.

"No. Who in their right mind would want to live on such a god forsaken place," the nameless lady spat toward me, then frowned when she realized how rude she had been. "My apologies. It's just been a while since I've killed someone and it's made me somewhat...restless."

...Okay. Make a mental note to never speak to her again. Now I didn't even want to know her name.

"What was your name again?" Jala asked me, running the flat end of her blade over her fingers. "I know you told me earlier but I forgot."

Probably because she didn't care. "Mary. And yours?"

"Jala."

"Nice to meet you." With that, I turned to my left with a hopeful expression.

"I refuse to give my name," Maddox stated, already seeing where this was going.

I smiled to myself. "Sure thing, Maddox."

The helmeted man glanced my way and, I'm assuming, frowned. "We will not get along."

"What is this? Elementary school?" The final woman, who still hadn't let her own title slip, leaned back in her leather seat and smirked. "We were hired to kill people, not have a meet and greet."

"And what's your name?" I interjected, unable to resist. This woman scared me half to death but I'd been around my husband for so long that I just couldn't resist making a jab like he would.

The woman glared at me, losing her patience. "My name is Zora and I refuse to go by anything else."

"That's okay. I'm not a nicknamer."

"Good."

On that note, about being hired to kill people, she was in for a big surprise. Derek Hacket hadn't hired us because he wanted us to murder other humans. (Technically he hadn't hired me at all. I'd come of my own free will but that was beside the point.) Honestly, no one knew what we were going to do once we reached the moon's space port.

I was in the midst of brainstorming new conversation starters when my earpiece started ringing. Smiling in embarrassment as both of the girls started to glare at me, I pressed the button on the side of the device and leaned away from them.

At least Maddox didn't seem to care about my phone call...He was probably listening to music inside that helmet anyway.

"Hello?"

"Mommy?"

"Yes?"

The little girl on the other end started screeching in excitement, forcing me to turn down the volume as best I could.

"Hey Polly," I said, grinning from ear to ear as she continued shrieking in excitement. We'd only been apart for five hours and she was already acting like a child. "How was school?"

"I drew a picture. See?"

"No, I can't." I giggled. She was turning eleven but still acted like a five year old. Her father spoiled her far too much. "Are you being good for Aunt Ebony?"

There was a pause. "I don't know. Aunt Ebony, am I being good?" she called to her babysitter/Valdis trainer.

"Yes, my dear," a soft, older voice answered from afar.

"See? I've been good."

"That's good." I was going to miss her but this mission had to come first. Plus, Polly was in very capable hands. Ebony was the sweetest woman I had ever met.

"Give Daddy a hug for me when you see him."

"I will."

"Okay, good. Bye bye. Love you!"

"I love you too," I answered with a goofy grin on my face. Then she hung up on me. So cute.

When I turned back to the others, Zora was giving me a look of disgust, Jala looked amused, and Maddox was expressionless because he had no face. Well, this would be a fun group to hang out with. They'd seemed so much cooler in the show.

"Hey! Mercenaries!" the pilot called back to us. "Look out the window! You can see the space port!"

Hearing that, I sat up and craned my head toward the window. Sure enough, off to our left was a huge ship of twisted metal and flashing lights hovering over the moon's surface. The word "Hikarius" was printed across its side in big, purple letters and I could see a few smaller ships rotating around it.

"Wow."

Eleven years of waiting. Eleven years of preparation and now I'd finally get to see the tales of Manica unfold! The adventure was beginning!

Chapter 22

Our ship was slowly inching its way into one of the ports when the pilot started muttering to himself, flipping a few switches with no response. "The station's oddly quiet," he informed us just in case we were curious. Then he added the frightening words: "Too quiet."

"Huh." I was considering probing for more information but jumped when I heard a loud thump to my left. The sound came from Maddox, who was loading a machine gun of some kind. The other two were doing the same, which made me feel left out since I'd only brought a tiny pistol just in case I needed to use it.

"If something's happened to Mr. Hacket then we need to make sure he's alive. Otherwise we'll never get paid," Jala informed us as she took a few cautious steps toward the ship's exit. "I'll head out first."

I watched as she shifted her weight from one foot to the other, impatient for the vehicle to land. They really saw Derek as nothing more than a money machine, didn't they?

"When you get inside, Hacket's AI will direct you," the pilot continued. "Just make sure to—"

The ship suddenly hit the ground midsentence and started screeching across the ground, the sound of metal scraping metal killing my ears. I barely had time to spot Jala jump off before the front of the ship collided with the end of the room and we were sent flying. I barely managed to avoid hitting my head on the hard floor, letting my arm take the blow instead which didn't feel much better.

As I sat on the floor, trying to pull my bruised body up, I heard an explosion behind me and turned to see the ship go up in flames. If the blow hadn't killed the pilot then the explosion definitely did.

"That hurt," I stated obviously as I got to my feet, still feeling a bit wobbly, and looked to see how the other three were doing. Not surprisingly, they were already armed and headed toward the nearest door.

"Welcome, hired mercenaries." Di's voice echoed inside my ear and I immediately sagged in relief. It was nice to hear a familiar voice. "Your employer is in trouble and needs your help. Please proceed to the door on your right."

I hurried to catch up with the others and drew my pistol. I'd been unsure about using a gun before but now I was too nervous not to. I took my position behind Maddox and followed the girls into the long, metal hallway looming before us.

"I have taken the liberty of locking all the doors except the ones you need to enter," Di told each of us over the speakers and in our ear pieces just in case the speakers were broken. "Please make haste. If you allow Derek Hacket to die he will withdraw your pay checks."

I laughed as we ran through the opened doors. Even Di was talking about cash.

As we traveled through the maze of completely empty hallways, which struck me as a little odd, I touched my earpiece and spoke quietly so none but Maddox could hear since he was right next to me but couldn't care less.

"Hi, Di. How are you?"

"I am doing fine," the computer informed me, not sounding excited about our reunion at all. "This is your first time on the moon station since Derek Hacket's promotion."

"Yup. How is he?"

"Surrounded."

"By what?"

"I do not know. For some reason I've lost control of all systems and security cameras within range of him."

If Di didn't even know what was going on then there was cause for alarm. "Di, why is the rest of the station completely empty?"

The computer paused, as though calculating how my reaction would affect the mission. Little did she know I already knew the answer. "You need to focus on locating Derek Hacket first."

Aw. She didn't trust me. "Okay, fine."

"I will end the conversation now."

The closer we got to our destination, the louder the sounds around us became. As we headed through the space station, a loud clicking and croaking mixed with mechanical booms kept echoing through the halls and it was sending chills down my spine. Even though I knew what was coming I still felt shivers climb up and down my pumping legs.

Maddox seemed to be listening to the sound too, though he was more focused on deciphering it than fearing it. I felt super relieved to have him next to me rather than those trigger happy girls.

It took a while but we eventually reached the origin of the sound.

As the four of us entered a large, empty room which only served as the entrance to yet another room, we found the answer to all our questions. The huge, steel door between us and that room was currently surrounded by five mysterious beings.

These creatures were surrounded by a bright blue mist and had glowing, white skin. Their bodies resembled those of women and had long, sapphire hair that served to cover their bodies, floating around them like rivulets of water. Their eyes were far larger than those of a human and the pupils were completely white, giving their faces an aura of death.

All four of us froze in the doorway when we saw them, raising our weapons but hesitant to fire. As we stared at them, watching them run their fingers over the doorway and lean over the body of a collapsed man, I started to worry that my heart might be loud enough for them to hear it.

The man lying on the ground in the fetal position was whimpering and had his eyes covered so he couldn't see the creatures standing above him.

"Should we wait?" Jala asked, glancing my way, her pistol already aimed at the nearest head. "That man's probably done for."

I shook my head. "If we hesitate they'll swallow his head whole and rip it from his shoulders," I whispered with a shudder, remembering how much that scene had traumatized me when I first saw it.

"Okay." Jala shrugged and fired, her bullet taking out a chunk of the first creature's head and sending it onto the floor. The creature made some sort snort sound before getting back up and turning toward us. It opened its mouth wide and the mechanical clicking got louder before being drowned out by our gunfire.

Both Jala and Maddox easily ran out of bullets and, almost in unison, dropped their empty guns and pulled out long swords. Jala's looked more ancient and had a dragon carved into the hilt while Maddox's was plain and thick. Without a moment of hesitation they ran into the midst of the monsters and started cutting their bodies in two, slicing off their glowing limbs.

I chose to stay in the doorway and continue shooting, which was a good thing and a bad thing. It kept me safe but my aim with a gun wasn't the best. I'd been practicing over the last couple years but only managed to hit my target fifty percent of the time. I had hoped it was an unnoticeable flaw but based on the looks Zora kept sending me, my amateur shooting was quite obvious.

Once all but one of the creatures were on the ground, shot to bits, Maddox called dibs on the final one and sliced his sword through its middle, cutting it in half before kicking its remains across the room.

The masked man then cleaned his sword with his arm and returned it to his back before stepping away from the hostage we'd rescued.

The weeping man continued to cover his head and might have stayed there forever if Zora hadn't nudged him with her foot.

"Hey! Get up or we leave you behind," Jala told him before examining the door the monsters had been trying to get through. As soon as she pressed her hand against its cold surface, the AI opened it for her.

As I joined the others, Maddox leaned toward the floor and examined one of the dead bodies. "What are these?" he asked, looking to us for answers.

"They are an alien lifeform native to the depths of the moon," Di informed us from the speakers above our heads. "They snuck aboard one of the drills and have spent the last five days eating 80% of the crew."

"What's a drill?" I asked, wanting more context.

"Mr. John Philips has been trying to drill into the moon's core for six months in the hopes of finding something valuable. Two months ago he discovered a—"

"Don't tell them anything!" the coward on the floor suddenly yelled, leaping to his feet and pointing at the ceiling as though that would somehow stop Di. "That is top secret information."

As soon as I realized who the guy was, I crossed my arms and raised an eyebrow. This man we'd just saved was John Philips, Derek's jerk of a boss. If I'd known it was him I might have considered letting him get eaten...Just kidding.

"Where's Derek Hacket?" Jala asked him expressionlessly, not caring who he was as he wasn't her source of income.

The middle aged man tried to brush off his rumpled, black suit and put his broken glasses back on the tip of his nose. I couldn't believe he hadn't invested in some better specs in ten years' time. "Last I saw him he was running off to the main control center. He's probably dead by now. That's where all the aliens are." He glanced at me, had a moment of realization about who I was, then frowned. "They're way smarter than they look. They might even try to land on Manica if you don't stop them."

"Then it's a good thing he hired us to come and help," Zora commented coldly as she stalked past him and stepped through the door. "And that we ignored your calls telling us not to accept the mission."

"Yes, well..." He scratched his head nervously, looking to me for help and receiving none. "I didn't want to place such important information in the hands of blood thirsty mercenaries."

"We definitely should have let him die," Jala whispered my way before continuing through the room toward our new destination.

I couldn't help but nod as we turned our walk into a run. If Derek was in trouble we had to hurry. There was a lot more than money at stake now.

Chapter 23

The clicking sound was starting up again and I had to resist plugging my ears because carrying a gun was more important. We'd been traveling through this maze of doors for almost half an hour and my legs were starting to ache. It was at times like this that I really wished I had the ability to fly...Sure, I could teleport but I didn't want to show off my powers to these people just yet.

"You are nearly there." Di's voice rang down from probably the biggest door we'd seen today. "There are a large number of enemies behind this door."

"Thanks for the warning but we're fine," Jala informed her, placing herself to the right of the entrance and holding up a gun she'd found earlier "Go ahead."

The AI obeyed and opened the control room. It was massive, nearly the size of a courtyard, and had a floor to ceiling window that looked out on the planet Manica and its surrounding stars. In front of the window was a large control panel that stretched about seven feet high. Surrounding it were twenty to thirty of those female aliens.

I desperately scanned the room for Derek but he was nowhere to be seen. My heart starting burning as I considered that he might already be dead but then a gunshot sounded from behind the control panel.

"Hey!" His voice sounded in our ears, his breath quick and labored. "Can you give me a little help, please? I've been holding these guys off for twenty minutes."

Maddox grabbed his sword and ran forward, silent as a cat and swift as a hawk. In moments he had cut off the head of the closest creature and was ready to dig into the rest.

As the girls went to join him I glanced over my shoulder at John Philips, who was attempting to hide behind the door as best he could. When he realized that he was being watched, he shooed me away and pointed to the crowd of aliens.

"Don't worry about me. Kill them!"

"I wasn't worried," I muttered under my breath, scrunching my nose at him before turning back to the fight. "I was just wondering why you wouldn't help us." Then, shaking my head, I also joined in...by shooting the aliens from afar.

Maddox and Jala were already starting to establish their trademark form of fighting. They were standing back to back and using their swords to slice their enemies' heads clean off. Maddox would dig his blade into the sternum of one and Jala would cut off the head while it was stabilized.

Zora was standing nearby and used two large pistols to demolish the enemy. Her aim was incredible, which made me slightly jealous, and she managed to land almost every shot near or in the enemy's brain, immediately rendering them helpless.

It was somewhat gruesome but also awesome to finally see the heroes of the story come to life.

When the last body fell, Derek finally peeked his head out from behind the control panel and breathed a loud, exaggerated sigh of relief. His black Hikarius uniform had some splatters of blood on it but he wasn't acting wounded so I allowed my panicked heart to calm down.

"Thank goodness you guys showed up," Derek yelled excitedly, his face lighting up as he holstered his equally blood covered gun and looked all three of them over. "Di definitely chose the right heroes for the job. I'm Derek Hacket."

Jala and Maddox were hesitant to shake his offered hand but Zora didn't seem to mind one bit. Her eyes were brighter than they'd been moments before which I could only hope was a result of killing crazy aliens, not from seeing my rugged, enthusiastic husband.

I had to admit, the years had been good to him. The scar on his face from ten years ago made him look more masculine and he'd started growing his hair out a little. I was kind of sad that Polly hadn't inherited his hair color because it looked really good on him and likely would have on her too. Instead, she'd grown up with blonde hair like mine.

Anyway, hair critiques aside, Derek was alive and looked super hyped about this adventure despite his entire crew getting killed by aliens.

"All right. Now I know that fighting aliens was not in the job description but, based on what I just saw, you guys should be able to handle it. I was originally going to send you straight to the moon's core to find out what's going on down there but, with the ship being attacked and all, that'll have to wait."

I found it kind of amusing that he hadn't noticed me yet. We hadn't seen each other for three weeks, after all. It was hard for him to convince his boss to let him visit Manica so our meetings had been few and far between. He was probably just distracted, right?

"I need your help to clear all of these...things out." He pointed to the corpses littering the ground with a look of disgust. "I've seen them eat lots of my coworkers. Once we get rid of them, we're gonna head down to the moon, find their hive or nest, and destroy it so they can't hurt anyone else."

Jala liked the sound of that but crossed her arms. "Who woke them up?"

Derek was about to answer when I spotted movement out of the corner of my eye. Since I was standing further away, I had a broader view of the room so when I looked up, I could see a final alien crawling along the corner of the ceiling, its arms digging into the wall paneling like a lizard of some kind. Its eyes were focused on Derek.

I knew what was about to happen. It was going to leap on top of him and try to rip him apart. I couldn't let that happen.

Yelling for everyone to duck, I raised my hand and flung the creature across the room, snapping its neck when it collided with the opposite wall. Then, to make sure it was truly dead, I sent it crashing onto the hard floor, breaking a few more of its bones.

"Whoa." Jala leapt backwards in surprise, laughing gleefully. "Are you a Valdis?"

I nodded, smiling slightly at her reaction, before turning back to Derek. He had finally noticed me.

His dark eyes were wide and I couldn't help but notice Zora's brow furrow as she watched him run toward me and wrap me in a tight hug, his laughter echoing through the huge room.

"What are you doing here?" he whispered, his face buried in my hair. "How are you? How's Polly?"

"We're all fine," I answered. "You're not injured, are you?"

"No." He hesitantly pulled away and took a look at the blood running down his front. "This was from a colleague of mine. He fell on top of me during the first attack a couple days ago. If it weren't for him I might have died."

I frowned, realizing I should have come earlier. I'd forgotten how early the aliens had invaded.

Seeing my concern, Derek gave me a quick kiss to assure me that everything was fine, then turned to the other three with a huge grin on his face. "Sorry for the interruption," he told them, just now realizing how embarrassing this must have been for them.

Both Zora and Jala looked slightly confused but Maddox was just staring out the window, oblivious and uncaring.

My husband chuckled, his sweet voice turning serious. "Mary is my wife so if you allow any harm to come to her I will kill you."

Chapter 24

"That's a bit harsh," I whispered, worriedly looking at the others to see if they'd been offended. His jokes were a bit too harsh and had gotten him in trouble many times.

"Sorry." Derek chuckled. "I was just trying to assert dominance. I'm just excited to see you again. Is Polly okay without you? I know she's been having trouble at school."

"She's fine, Derek. I really think we need to focus on the issue at hand, though." I loved Polly, don't get me wrong, but by keeping Derek safe I would indirectly be keeping Polly safe.

"You're right." He released my hand and led the group toward the giant computer he'd previously been using as a hiding place. "Those things have been blocking my access to certain sections of the station so I came here in an attempt to get them back online. Unfortunately there's a passcode to get in so I'll need you four to find it and bring it back here so we can regain control of the ship."

Even though I knew he was trying to dumb down his words for us I still had no clue what he was talking about.

"How do we find it?" Zora asked, allowing her poker face to return.

"My friend Ace programmed it and he's locked himself inside one of the safe rooms along with four other engineers. You'll need to find him, bring him here, and escort the other four to a working ship so they can return to Manica and get help. We've lost all communications with the planet. Di barely managed to contact you three before we were blocked off."

"Is Ace doing okay?" I asked. Derek's best friend had seemed somewhat hesitant about moving into space and now he'd be able to say "I told you so" to us.

"He's fine but won't be for long if we lose control of the ship. I'm counting on you guys." He cast each of them a reassuring smile before glancing my way for a split second. "I'm not sure if I want you going, though."

"I'll be fine. I'm a Valdis."

He raised an eyebrow. We both knew that he was talking about the alternate reality in which his wife died but I refused to believe it would happen. "I'll be extra careful," I reassured him. We'd managed to not kill his grandma, though she died of a heart attack a year later, so I believed we could save my life too. And his. And Polly's.

Derek hesitated, drawing in a breath to say something before releasing it and nodded, putting his faith in me. "I'll lock myself in here and do what I can to help you, which isn't much."

"We can handle it," Jala answered, eager to go.

"What about me?" John Philips suddenly popped out from behind the door and jogged toward us, sweat pouring down his face despite not participating in any of the action. "I can't go with them!"

Derek shot him a look of annoyance, clearly hoping that he'd died in the attack, before looking away, his left eye twitching slightly. "... You can...stay in here with me so long as you don't touch anything."

"As your boss I have the right to—"

"You...!" Derek reached for my hand and started squeezing it again, veins popping out on his arms. "You are the reason all of my men are dead. If you dare to touch anything I will send you out to deal with the problem you created, is that understood Sir?" He emphasized the sir darkly.

John stepped back, insulted, but nodded, squinting at him through his glasses. "Fine. But if I know you're doing something wrong don't think I'll hesitate let you know about it."

"I know," Derek whispered, shooting me one last look of desperation before letting go and walking toward the control panel. I took one more moment of watching him roll up his sleeves and start pressing buttons before I finally followed the heroes out the door.

"I love you," I heard him say through my earpiece before he locked himself in. "Please don't die."

"Same to you," I said, making sure to sound confident. The only ones who had a chance of dying today were those aliens and maybe John Philips. Not us. We could change the story. We would. I had to keep telling myself that, otherwise I'd stop blindly believing it.

Chapter 25

Maddox was the first to reach the safe room. He was the stealthiest out of all of us and, when he peeked around a corner and saw a pair of aliens guarding the door, he motioned for me to join him.

"You are a Valdis," he stated without continuing. Luckily for him, I understood what he meant and nodded, pulling out a small knife. I wasn't sure why we needed to go the stealthy route but had nothing to lose so I went with it.

Squinting in concentration, I weighed the blade in my hand then stepped forward, teleporting behind the female creatures and immediately driving the blade into one of their heads. I then teleported behind the second's back, giving her a second to see her companion fall before stabbing her too.

Too easy.

As the girls joined us once more, Maddox gave me a nod of approval which filled my insides with warmth. Next to Derek, Maddox's approval was what I had always dreamed of.

"Ace?" I knocked on the door as loudly as I could in the hopes that he could hear me. "It's Mary. Derek sent me to find you."

There was a moment of silence, then someone knocked back and the door slid into the ceiling. Standing before me was an older Ace and four young, frightened engineers dressed in blue uniforms and wearing helmets for protection. Every one of them had a Hikarius machine gun in their hands.

"Hey, Mary," Ace greeted me as though my presence was to be expected. "Sorry for not coming out earlier. I couldn't put these guys' lives as risk."

I nodded, understanding completely. "Not a problem. Let's go before that happens." I knew Ace could handle himself in a fight. His father had been a police officer in the past, though Ace had apparently never seen himself actually using the training that had been forced upon him as a child.

As we headed back with Ace, Maddox, and I in the front, Jala and Zora guarding the back, and the useless technicians in the middle, Ace started giving orders to Di.

"I wasn't able to contact her in there," he told me quietly after he'd given Di all the hard to understand information she'd needed. "Those aliens are really messing with our systems."

This had been the point in the show when I'd just nodded and acted like I understood. I was doing that now. "Of course."

"You don't know what I'm talking about, do you?"

"I know what 'systems' means but the stuff before that just went over my head."

Ace just laughed. "It's fine. I don't expect people to comprehend it unless they've gone to school like I have. Don't worry."

"Oh. Maddox should know, though, right?" I looked past Ace at the helmeted man who simply shrugged and kept walking. He likely just didn't care enough to bother talking out loud.

"Are these the mercs Derek hired?" Ace asked, glancing over his shoulder at the black haired women behind us. "It's a good thing they came. Kind of wish there were more, though."

"We'll be fine. These guys can survive anything." Literally. In chapter 87, which was way farther than the show had ever gone, they'd literally survived an explosion in space. How they managed to have a fire without oxygen was beyond me but...Yeah. The creators had really started trying to one up themselves. That was part of the reason I hadn't told Derek about the comics.

"Are they coming to the moon with us?"

I nodded. I couldn't wait to get inside the moon!

"Okay. Good. But let's not get ahead of ourselves. We should focus on gaining control of the station first."

"Of course." I nodded. Ace was so level headed. I don't how we would have survived without him.

As we walked I noticed that he kept glancing back at our new companions, particularly in Jala's direction. The girl kept ignoring his stares on purpose but I couldn't help but giggle inside. I had been shipping them since the beginning of the series.

"She's pretty, isn't she?"

He nodded hesitantly.

"Wanna talk to her?" I asked, nudging him like an annoying old woman.

Ace just shook his head, keeping a straight face. "I'm too old for her."

"I'm sure she won't care."

"I have a mission to focus on, Mary."

"You're right." He was always right. I was getting too distracted. I'd just been waiting too long for this to happen and couldn't resist getting excited but this next week was the most crucial part of my life and I needed to stay focused. But... "Maybe later then?" I whispered with a hopeful grin.

He sighed, then shot me a rare look of annoyance. "Later."

"Good." I'd always felt that they'd needed a push toward a relationship and never got one so I planned to fulfil that need.

I was about to continue when Maddox suddenly thrust his sword in front of Ace and I, stopping us in our tracks. My eyes lingered on the blade before looking past it and seeing what had alarmed him.

Standing before us with its lumbering back turned was an alien far larger than any we'd encountered before. It resembled a white blob and the tip of its head nearly brushed against the ceiling. Its legs were like those of a fish and were sprawled out before it in a relaxed position. From the looks of it, blades and bullets wouldn't do much to penetrate its fat and lumpy body.

I glanced at Jala, fear in my eyes.

Should we fight or flee?

Chapter 26

"All right." Jala pushed through the engineers and stood between us, surveying the obstacles and escape routes between us and the blob of shining goop. "Ace, you and Zora escort these men to Derek Hacket's safe room while Maddox, the Valdis, and I distract the beast."

Why did they keep calling Derek by both names and why was I "the Valdis" instead of Mary?

"Understood." Ace gestured for the men to follow him and they snuck along the wall to the right with Zora taking up the rear. Meanwhile, I looked to Maddox and Jala to see if they had a plan of attack.

Jala examined the room once more, then nudged my shoulder and pointed to the metal box of unknown contents off to our left. "Drop that on its head," she whispered before nodding to Maddox and ducking behind cover.

I took a moment to breathe, keeping an eye on the escapees, before focusing all my attention on lifting the heavy box and silently bringing it to hover over the monster's head or at least what I thought was its head. I let it hang there for a second, bit my lip, then let it fall as soon as Ace reached the door.

The box came down with a resounding crash and caused the thing to moan but, as soon as my attack slid off its now misshapen head it turned toward me with a roar. Where its eyes should have been were two gaping holes trailing down into its stomach and its arms were short like a t-rex's. It really reminded me of a ghost.

"Get out of the way!" Jala warned me moments before it slid forward, not even bothering to use its legs, and brought its face down toward me in an attempt to swallow me whole. I had only one second to teleport to the other side of the room before it smooshed its eyes and mouth into the shiny floor.

As I turned back to assess the damage, Maddox climbed atop the fallen box and used it as a step to jump on the creature's back. He then started cutting chunks of its smooth body and launching them across the room. Contrary to how it looked, the alien was not slimy and therefore somewhat easy for the man to latch onto with his padded gloves.

"Stand back," Jala warned as she approached the thing, tossing a red grenade up and down in her hand. "This could get messy."

She always said such cheesy lines. I loved it.

I felt my heart leap as soon as I saw Ace enter the room, then felt it drop just as quickly when Mary didn't come in him. As I ran toward them, ignoring John who was sitting nearby doing nothing helpful whatsoever, I had to keep myself from demanding what happened.

"Hey, Derek." Ace gave me a quick hug before heading toward the control panel. "Your wife stayed behind to fight a monster," he explained, already knowing I'd be worried about her whereabouts. "She should be here in a few minutes."

"Thanks." I tried to act relieved but wasn't. As he ran toward the front of the room, focused on his job, I stayed back and made sure the door was securely locked behind us. I couldn't risk another alien getting inside.

As I pressed on the door to make sure it was secure, the long haired merc I'd hired, Zora I believe, walked up beside me.

"So." She nodded at me then subtly pointed in my boss' direction. "If he's the one who set these aliens loose, why do you still keep him around?"

I chuckled. She'd read my mind. "I'm kind of hoping he'll get killed before he can cause any more trouble," I joked. "Seriously, though, I can't just kill someone because they're an idiot. If I did that a lot of people would be dead."

"Did you wife tell you that?"

That was an odd question. "No. I just figured it was true. Technically, all of us are stupid in one way or another so I guess..." I trailed off, realizing how much I sounded like an old man. I guess it was partly true, though, since I was already in my mid-thirties.

The woman looked away, her eyes clouded, and I started to wonder if she wanted to quit.

"If you have any qualms about this mission you are more than welcome to go back to Manica with the rest of the crew. I can still pay you—"

"No!" she suddenly yelled before she lowered her voice, catching me off guard. "I'm not a coward. I enjoy killing so it's fine."

"Really? That's a bit...odd." My mind flashed back to the "me" I'd seen in the show who had also reveled in murder. It was not a mindset I ever wanted to bear. "Were you...brought up as an assassin or...?"

"I killed my parents...and my adoptive parents...and both of my bosses...and two of my ex-boyfriends..." She crossed her arms and smirked. "The world hasn't treated me kindly so I've returned the favor."

I wanted to shiver but held back. Now I wished she would go back on that ship to Manica. "Does it...make you feel better?"

"No but I value revenge. I think people deserve what they've got coming to them. So if that boss of yours' ever gives you any trouble..." She pulled a finger across her throat while smiling at me as though she was doing me a favor.

"Uh...Thanks." I scratched my head nervously before walking away, cringing as soon as my back was turned. What a colorful past she had. Were the other two newcomers just as bad?

As I joined my best friend and lingered next to him, trying to pretend that I was watching him work, I felt the girl's eyes boring into my back. I really hoped she didn't like me or anything. She reminded me too much of my alternate self.

"You okay?" Ace asked, glancing my way with his hands frozen on one of the panels.

I nodded and chuckled nervously. "Yeah. Never been better."

"...Okay." He blinked, then continued his job. "Nice to have Mary back, huh?"

"Yeah." I couldn't wait to have her back by my side. Maybe she'd scare away that other woman. Her blue eyes held more death in them than those monsters' pupil-less ones did.

Chapter 27

"Okay, everyone keep a sharp eye out for aliens and stay together," Jala ordered the engineers as she passed between them, her pretty eyes glaring at them to ensure they obeyed. "If one of you gets lost we're not gonna risk our lives to come and find you, understood?"

I sat by and watched as they psyched themselves up for the escape mission. If I didn't have my Valdis powers I'd probably be like those men, afraid and helpless. As a result I couldn't blame them for feeling that way.

"Are you sure you can't stay here?" Derek whispered, wrapping his fingers around my arm as we watched the lecture.

I tilted my head and looked into his eyes. It was cute to see him acting so protective, made me care for him all the more, but I wanted to make sure everyone was okay. "I'll be fine, Derek. I survived the last mission."

"I know but..." His eyes darted from my face to the group and back to me again. "I'm just worried. I don't want the story to come true."

"It won't," I whispered, forcing a confidence I didn't really feel. In the hopes of making him less nervous I pulled his face down slightly and kissed him, hoping no one was watching because that would make it awkward for everyone.

As he pulled away, his expression was steeled. "You never kiss me in public." He'd taken that as a sign that something really was wrong.

I shook my head. "Nothing is wrong, Derek. Listen, if you're that worried just talk to me on the comms, okay? I'll be sure to answer."

"Great. Then if you die, I can hear it crystal clear. Thanks...I love you."

My heart melted like the silly fangirl I'd become. That was two times in one day he'd said that. I was about to respond when Maddox tapped my shoulder and nodded toward the door before following the group as they exited.

I smiled and gave Derek one more kiss before running after the others. "I'll be back!" I called and waved before Di shut the door, locking Derek and Ace inside for the last time. The next time we saw them we'd be heading into the moon.

It was kind of sad having to see that crashed ship again since it reminded me of the pilot who had died inside it but my sadness was easily diminished when we spotted some aliens and had to get rid of them so the men could get through.

Lucky for us, there were a couple ships in working order and all of the engineers knew how to fly one so there was no need to worry. As Jala ordered them onto the one in the best physical condition,

Maddox, Zora, and I stood guard, keeping an eye out for more of those white females.

Luckily my past experience with the ceiling made me keep an eye on it and I managed to catch one lone creature trying to sneak across it, crawling on all fours in an attempt to camouflage itself. It didn't work.

Frowning, I flicked it off the ceiling like one would a bug and sent it flying out of the purple force field protecting us from the outside. As it spun away through space, its arms flailing before becoming motionless, I wondered how possible it would be for that alien to hit Manica. I mean, this moon was way closer to the planet than Earth's moon was.

"Nice," Zora complimented me with a grin as she watched the creature turn into nothing more than a dot. "Wish I'd thought of that."

I grinned. Maybe she wasn't so bad after all.

"Good to go." Jala knocked on the back of the ship and we all watched as it inched out of the station and flew back to Manica, carrying the remaining survivors home. I'm sure they never planned to come back here.

"All right." Jala finally joined us and placed her hands on her hips, looking satisfied with their work today. "Ready to go back?"

Maddox didn't need another invitation and immediately walked back the way we'd come, shaking his head as though he was insulted she'd asked.

When we entered the control room Ace and Derek were standing off against John. My husband's face was contorted in anger, his face turning a light pink and his eyes blazing with fury. Ace didn't look quite as angry but his mouth was hanging open out of worry.

Across from them, John was examining the computer with a blissful smile on his face. He looked ready to start fiddling with the machine when we walked in, the four of us forming a line around the three, not sure what we'd walked in on.

"John," Ace began, keeping his voice level and his eyes trained on his boss. "We need you to stay on the ship...where you're safe. Di will take care of the station while we're gone."

"But I'm the leader of the expedition. I should come down to—"

"No!"

My eyes went wide at the rage in Derek's voice. It had dropped and octave lower and as soon as he'd yelled it, he'd looked away, staring at me with desperation in his eyes. He hadn't meant to say that out loud.

"Derek." I dropped my voice too and grabbed his arm, pulling him toward the side door as quickly and subtly as I could. We needed to get out before he said something he'd regret. "We'll be right back," I managed to tell the others before shutting the door behind us.

As soon as we were alone he started running his hands through his hair, walking the length of the hall and clenching and unclenching his fists, looking ready to punch the wall.

"He wants to come to the moon...again," he told me, his muscles rippling with each word. "Last time he came, he unleashed an army of aliens that killed every living soul on this ship. We warned him the first time to be careful and he didn't listen. Now, he wants to do it again and we won't just sit by and watch as he—"

"Okay." I grabbed one of his arms, trying to bring warmth into my voice. "I'll talk to him. I'll make sure he stays here."

"Sometimes I just want to strangle him," Derek hissed, wringing his hands nervously. "I could just say that the aliens did it..."

I gulped. I hadn't heard this tone in his voice for years. "Derek, we talked about this. Killing John will hurt you far more than it could ever hurt him." It technically wasn't true but to us it was.

"I know but..." He turned to me with puppy eyes. "I knew some of the men on this ship. Some of them were my best friends. And he just...he doesn't even care. I mean, look at him!"

I nodded, knowing all too well how much of a pain John Philips was. I didn't want to admit it but I'd felt relief when he'd died in the show. But his murder, which had technically been Dark's second kill because he'd refused to let him into the control room and had let him die, only brought him closer to the darkness that led to his and Polly's death. I couldn't allow that to happen.

"I know how hard it is," I whispered, seeing his shoulders drop when I spoke. "But I beg you to protect yourself. And...if worse comes to worse, I'll kill him for you."

"What?" His eyes shot to mine in disbelief. "I can't let you—"

"Better I than you," I told him, trying to show a confidence I didn't feel. "I'll ensure he stays on the ship and we'll deal with the threat on the moon together. We already know how to stop them so there shouldn't be any more casualties." I was still disappointed in myself for being too late to save the rest of the ship's crew. "I promise."

My husband nodded, resting his head on my shoulder and blinking a few times in an attempt to calm himself down. "Okay. I..." He took a deep breath. "I trust you."

"Thank you Derek." I smiled. "I trust you too." I trusted him to control himself and not become the monster he was destined to be. "Now let's go to the moon."

Chapter 28

Di was the one who drove our small, black ship onto the moon's surface but Derek stayed behind the wheel just in case something went wrong again. Both he and Ace knew how to pilot ships but rarely got the chance since they were stuck behind computers all day.

The blank and grey moon that orbited earth looked nothing like this moon. This one was the color of black death and its surface consisted of jagged, solid rocks and crevices, forming mountains, caves, and tunnels that ran around its insides like a series of subways.

It had taken years for Hikarius to actually reach the moon's core, which was where the aliens had been sleeping before John's accidentally woke them up. Every ounce of their technology had been locked away in there and he'd been so desperate to get at it that he'd broken in without adequate preparation, which was his and the rest of Hikarius' employees' downfall.

I was the only one feeling apprehensive about this because the three mercenaries took everything in stride and Ace and Derek had already been down here before. They were readying their weapons as though they were about to go out on patrol, not to fight pale, eyeless creatures of unknown origin.

"Follow the purple lights," Derek told us as he stepped off the ship onto the mist covered ground, a Hikarius machine gun balanced in his hands. The bullets of light it fired were violet in color and could melt the face off a human. "And keep an eye out for the aliens. This is their territory so they could be hiding anywhere."

"And make sure not to damage any of their technology," John's voice rang over our earpieces, making every one of us cringe and press the mute button. "If you—"

"All right. Let's get in, destroy their nest, and get out," Jala stated as she followed Derek, shooting us glares before taking a look at her surroundings. "I don't want to be down here any longer than necessary."

I slammed my fists together to psych myself up, which Zora shot me a weird look for, before strapping on my oxygen helmet and leaping off the end of the ship at the same time Maddox did. My knees buckled a little when I landed but other than that I was okay. I still didn't have a weapon in hand but figured there were enough rocks around here to serve as weapons.

Just like Derek had said, there was a continuous row of magenta lights leading us through the maze of towering stone. They'd been planted there by the engineers who had either escaped or been eaten earlier.

Things felt eerily quiet as we passed through the layers of stone, which I knew were actually tombs of the previous alien generations because of the comics, and I felt a shiver run down my spine as we proceeded. The farther down we went, the colder it started to feel. Soon it was so frigid that I could feel the cold covering my skin like moisture. It was uncomfortable.

"I like this place," Zora characteristically commented as she spun around, taking a look at the environment. "Feels like a superhero cave."

Hearing that made me wonder if they had a comic book hero similar to batman in Manica. Hmm. If I'd cared about him instead of Dark, could I have teleported to his world instead? I guess I'd never know.

The more time we spent walking without an attack of any kind the more nervous I became.

"We're almost there," Derek whispered as the tunnel walls started glowing. "Their home is hidden in the deepest tunnels and they're even more hostile down there. I think it's where they hide their children."

My heart started to shrink at the thought of killing babies but I knew it would be self-defense of a sort and therefore couldn't be helped. As I stayed at my husband's side, my hands started to twitch out of anticipation for a battle.

At first, the walls locking us in were flat and colorless, something that likely would have driven a claustrophobic person insane. But as we continued toward the light I started to get the sense that the walls were watching us, shifting slightly and wishing that we'd leave.

Out of the corner of my eye, I saw Maddox raise his weapon and shoot at one of the walls, an action I thought was odd until I saw a black skinned alien fall away from it, Maddox's bullet lodged in his abdomen.

As soon as they realized what had happened, the aliens attacked, launching themselves off their hiding spots on the walls and trying to tear at our flesh. Their white eyes stood out from their now sickly, black skin and it made them appear even more frightening than the albino ones had looked. Could they camouflage themselves in any color?

Panicking, I used my telekinesis on one of the aliens and flung it against another, my eyes going wide as the wild creatures surrounded us, hissing and clicking their tongues before trying to tear off our limbs. Derek had been right. These ones were far more territorial. Perhaps they were the 'Mother' aliens who cared for the young. Mother bears were said to be more defensive when their children were around, after all.

Maddox dug his sword through one of the alien's sides, lodging it in its flesh before ripping it out and driving it into another. Jala kicked one out of the way before stabbing it in the chest, her mouth pursed in concentration.

Once it was clear that we were outnumbered, Zora pulled out the large machine gun she'd had strapped to her back and spewed a stream of bullets into the horde, lowering the playing field and giving us an opening. As soon as Derek noticed the tunnel emptying, he grabbed my hand and tugged me toward the glow.

"We won't have much time before reinforcements come," he told everyone as we ran. "Let's hurry." He glanced at Ace to make sure he still had the explosives strapped to his arms, which they planned to use on the alien nests, before continuing.

The mercs took care of any stragglers as Derek, Ace, and I entered the aliens' "control room".

The room we entered was maybe the size of my bedroom times three. Small pods were lining the walls and I'm guessing they were full of incomplete alien children or eggs of some kind. The emerald glow we'd been seeing in the tunnels was coming from the biggest pod situated at the back of the room. Unlike the others, this one was clear, allowing us to peer inside.

Resting in the middle of the pod, with her eyes closed and arms crossed like a corpse, rested a white skinned alien. Her skin glowed green and her hair was swirling around the top of the pod, weaving back and forth like ripples in a pond.

"It's the mother," I found myself whispering.

She looked so peaceful...and we were going to kill her.

Chapter 29

Ace and Derek were attaching their sticky explosives to the pods, setting the timers to a few minutes so we'd have enough time to escape the blast radius. As they did that, I approached the mother's pod, feeling my heart warm from the kindness and fear in her face.

As I pressed my hand against the warm, vibrating surface of the pod, my mind traveled back to the events that had transpired before we'd arrived. John Philips had shot one of the pods when Derek was having a look at them and it had awakened the aliens, putting them on the defensive.

My question was: what if John hadn't done that? Would Derek and the scientists of Hikarius have been able to communicate with the aliens and get along with them? Could they have joined forces and made the world a better place?

I clenched my fist. If I hadn't been so hesitant about leaving Polly behind, I might have gotten here earlier and could have stopped John.

I could have even warned John about it instead but had forgotten. This was all my fault.

As I watched the mother, blocking out the sound of the two men as they rushed back and forth across the room, I stared into her peaceful, sleeping face. She had no idea what was about to happen.

"I am so sorry," I whispered, leaning my forehead against the pod and sighing. "If I hadn't been so selfish I might have remembered to save you too. I'm sorry."

As I stared at her, my insides tightening, a single tear slipped down her cheek. She was starting to slowly open her eyes and turn her giant, black pupils toward me when Derek grabbed my arm and tried to pull me back into the tunnels.

"Mary, we have to go! The timers have started."

"No!" My fingers stretched out toward the creature, her eyes droopy and her expression one of surrender. "I think I can talk to her. I think—"

"Her 'people' killed my men!" Derek yelled as he pulled me into his arms and resisted my struggles. "They can't be negotiated with."

"I saw it in her eyes!" I screamed as we ran past the mercenaries, who gave us one glance before realizing what was happening and dashing after us.

"You can't save everyone, Mary," Derek whispered, already sounding regretful. "It's too late. The bombs can't be disabled."

"And by killing one person," Ace added, referring to the mother, "We can save millions on Manica. The needs of the many outweigh the needs of the few."

Knowing they were right, I stopped trying to go back and allowed my husband to hide me behind some of the biggest rocks in the tunnels. The others did the same and prepared for the blast, covering their heads with their faces.

As I sat there, breathing heavily and waiting for the loud boom that would soon rock the moon, my mind rocked back and forth between the 'what ifs' of the past and those of the present. Was there a way for me to save them now? I could teleport there but wouldn't know how to disable the bombs and even if I did the aliens might already be too hostile to negotiate with now.

I squeezed Derek's hands between mine and shut my eyes as the bombs exploded and sent searing heat through the tunnels, warming up the rocks we were leaning against and burning the edges of my hair.

As the flames continued to fly past us, Derek pulled me against his chest and held me tight. He probably regretted this more than I did unlike Dark who had likely enjoyed it.

Dark couldn't help but chuckle to himself as he crouched behind the rock, alone, and counted down the seconds before the explosion. He couldn't wait to blow those monsters back into the hole they'd crawled out of.

58 57 56.

"Sir." Di's voice echoed in his ear.

"What is it Di?"

"...It's about your wife, sir."

"What about her?" Dark asked. She should still be on Manica with Polly.

Ace looked up from his hiding spot, Maddox and Jala by his side. The best friend frowned when he saw Dark's face pale and his eyes darken, his fists clenching before wrapping around the earpiece.

"What?!?"

His yell was immediately drowned out by the explosion and all four of them were forced to duck behind the security of their stones, covering their heads and gritting their teeth as the heat of the blast brushed past them.

Once the flames subsided and were replaced with a thick layer of black smoke, Dark leapt to his feet and threw the earpiece on the ground, crushing it under his boot before whirling around, unsure what he should do.

"Dark...What's wrong?" Ace hesitantly stood, brushing off his pants as he approached the enraged man. "What did Di say?"

Dark turned to him with tears in his eyes. "My wife she...she's dead."

"What? How?"

"I don't know. She..." He turned his gaze toward the explosion, a million expressions flying across his face. "I just talked to her yesterday on the phone. I don't know why she'd..." He finally broke down. "She was all I had!"

"Well, technically you still have your daughter," Jala offered, unaware of how sarcastic and cruel she sounded to his ears.

His face contorted into a scowl and he punched one of the steaming rocks, the skin on his knuckles blistering from the burns. Whirling toward the two mercenaries, who weren't quite grasping the situation, he pointed a burnt finger at them. "You think this is funny?" he yelled. "What do you know about my wife or me for that matter? She was so delicate and tried so hard to cover up her insecurities with a hard exterior. She was the only woman I ever learned to love and now she's gone forever!"

"To you, my wife was just a number. A toy to be played around with," he continued. "People like you are the ones who destroyed her. She was beaten and abused and molested and had no one to love her but me and—"

"Dark." Ace grabbed his arms, trying to pull him away from Maddox and Jala. "They didn't say anything against your wife. You're just trying to vent your anger—"

"Shut up, Ace!" Tears continuing streaming down his face as he punched his friend in the face and shoved him against one of the walls.

Ace grunted when he landed on his arm and heard a painful snap. Moaning, he gritted his teeth before looking back at Dark, who was kicking the walls and throwing as many rocks around as he could. His muscles were rippling and his eyes were beginning to burn red as they darted back and forth, mirroring the wild thoughts zipping inside his head.

"Ace," Jala whispered, pulling him to his feet and leading him away from Dark. "He's lost it. We need to leave."

"No," Ace protested, loosely holding up his broken arm. "There's only one ship down here. If we leave him now he'll be stranded."

"Better than letting him kill us," Jala answered, glancing one last time at the broken man as he stalked down the tunnels toward the remains of the alien control room. "I don't know if I can win in a fight with him."

Maddox nodded, already sheathing his sword and turning toward ship.

"But...he's my friend."

"If he'd thrown you any harder you might have cracked your skull," Jala whispered in his ear, growing tired of his protests. "He tried to kill you, Ace, and no longer deserves your pity. Now, we need to go!"

The blond continued to shake his head but allowed himself to be dragged back down the tunnel, his eyes trained on Dark's back as the villain entered the cave, his broad shoulders straight and head held high. This was the last time they'd see each other on the same side.

This was the final betrayal.

First the grandmother. Then John Philips. Then his wife. Then his friends and allies.

What Jala didn't know was that Di could send another ship to pick up her master after he was abandoned. He wouldn't be stranded here and when he came back, his fury would be stronger than ever.

Chapter 30

Once we were sure the heat was no longer strong enough to kill us we crept out from our hiding spots and reentered the tunnel, eager to see what was left behind. It took a lot of willpower for Derek and me not to discuss what we knew we'd find.

All of the pods had shattered and were scattered around the floor of the cave, their remains floating through the air in specks of green dust. I started coughing when I first stepped in and had to swallow several times before the dry taste of sugar left the back of my throat.

At the back of the room, where the mother had been, there was yet another, smaller tunnel leading further into the moon. Its entrance had been blocked earlier by the pod, a design choice that was likely intentional. Now, we were free to go down and see what the aliens had been hiding. Maddox was the only one who kept his gun close as we entered the darkness.

As we walked, the glowing dust that came down with us serving as our only source of light. They were swirling around like fireflies.

Maybe the specks weren't following us but were actually drawn to whatever was down there.

Finally, the tunnel ended and imbedded in the wall at the end was a small, green ball of light. It was sitting in the center of the rock and when Derek reached toward it, it started to glow brighter, lighting up the rest of the tunnel.

"What is it?" Ace whispered, making sure not to touch it just in case it was dangerous. He was more cautious than Derek, who immediately touched it, running his fingers over its cold surface.

Forgetting that he wasn't supposed to know information about the future, Derek answered him. "It's the alien's life force. It keeps them alive and gives them their shapeshifting abilities." He was referring to the blobs we'd fought in the ship, which had actually been multiple females morphed together to form that creature.

"Then we should destroy it," Jala stated nonchalantly, wanting to eradicate the aliens as quickly as possible so she could get paid.

Derek shook his head. "You don't understand. The aliens never harnessed this ball's full potential. We could use this to power everything in Manica. We could create weapons of world peace and space ships that go beyond the moon. The possibilities are endless."

"Then let's grab it and go," Zora ordered, shuffling back toward the exit. "Before the aliens come back."

Derek nodded and wrapped his fingers around the orb. He gritted his teeth and tugged but it stayed put. It wasn't until he yelled and yanked that the sphere popped out, its glow disappearing as he hid it inside his pocket coat and turned toward me.

I was about to smile when the ground shifted beneath our feet and a loud creak echoed down the tunnel, catching us off guard.

Derek smirked, already expecting this, and grabbed my hand, dashing down the tunnel and ignoring the rocks that came crashing down around our feet. The others weren't far behind.

"I hope, for all our sakes, that wasn't the thing holding this moon together," Ace yelled as we ran for our lives.

The ship was already hovering and prepared for lift off when we reached it. Di must have realized something was wrong and was waiting for us. As soon as we reached the ship I leapt inside, pulling Derek with me. I could have teleported us out of the tunnels but we hadn't been in that much immediate danger so I'd held off just in case something went wrong.

Once everyone was inside, Di flew us from the moon moments before a crack crawled across ground we'd been standing on moments before. The moon would survive this earthquake-like phenomenon but going back on in would be too risky from now on. Not that it mattered now. All future excitement would happen on the space ship and Manica from now on.

As we sat down, using the break to catch our breath and watch the cracks shoot across the moon like zebra stripes, I glanced at Derek and laughed quietly, my tense body loosening from the adrenaline.

My husband returned the smile, his eyes shining before he looked down and pulled the small orb out of his pocket to examine it. It didn't look like much as he tossed back and forth in his hands but we both knew the power it possessed.

In the alternate story, Dark had combined it with Polly's powers to control a world destroying weapon but we had other plans this time. With this, Manica could become even more advanced than Earth was or ever would be. We could make it a better, safer place and I couldn't wait.

No one else on the ship knew what we knew. None of them knew that we'd just managed to dodge every single level of betrayal Dark had faced. Other than those of the aliens', Derek didn't have any blood on his hands.

I had done it. I had saved Dark Hacket.

I had succeeded.

And when he looked at me with the expression of an excited child, my heart felt ready to burn up. I was so glad I'd been sent here and I never wanted to leave. I loved this man so much and couldn't wait to see him and Polly reunited once more.

Chapter 31

We were all excited when we reached the control room, the mercs because they thought they were getting paid and me because I had finally changed the fate of a fictional world. It had taken ten years to do so but I was thrilled about it.

Unfortunately, John Philips was not.

As soon as we entered the room he whirled toward us with a red face and bulging eyes and pointed to one of the computer screens, his hands shaking. "A piece of the station fell off a few minutes ago."

"What?" Ace ran forward to investigate and immediately started searching the security cameras to see where the damage was done. "...I have to go take a look. Will you guys be fine on your own?" he asked as he ran toward the door, a gun in one hand and a tool box in the other.

"Wait." Derek grabbed his arm as he passed. "Take some of the mercs with you. There could still be aliens hiding in there."

Ace shrugged and barely paid attention to Maddox and Jala as they joined him. They were far from happy about completing yet another escort mission.

Once they were gone, John spoke up again. "And another thing! This entire ship is falling apart! I refuse to stay here any longer and demand I be taken back to Manica. The AI says there's already a ship waiting."

I could tell my husband was doing all he could not to roll his eyes. "Fine. Zora will escort you to the hangar since you obviously won't go alone." He glanced at Zora to verify, who nodded with a frown on her face.

"Good." Derek was about to head toward the computers when his boss spoke up once more.

"It seems unfair that Ace gets two people to escort him while I only get one."

Geez. Was this guy a two year old?

Rolling my eyes on purpose, since my husband couldn't, I stepped forward and pulled out my pistol. "Fine. I'll come too." I shot Derek an apologetic look, which he returned, before following the wimp out of the control room, my moment of victory forgotten.

The hangar looked the same. Nothing had shifted other than one, small ship which Di must have moved. It was sitting on the edge of the force field leading out into space.

As I walked toward it, keeping an eye out for any aliens, though I was sure the removal of the sphere had gotten rid of any remaining ones, I glanced back at Zora and John, who were standing side by side behind me.

I was just within touching distance of the tiny, silver ship built for two when I heard Zora whisper something to my husband's boss.

"Shoot the camera in the far left corner," she told him, her order so quiet that I had to strain to listen. It didn't fully register in my brain until John picked up the small gun she had handed him, looked at the black camera hanging off the ceiling, and shot at it. His first two shots missed but the third cracked the screen, causing it to power down.

"Hmm?" I threw my hands up in confusion as Zora approached me. "What are you doing?"

"This guy's nuts," she whispered, grabbing my arm and pulling me away from John, who was now looking at us with mounds of confusion on his face.

I was even more baffled. "You know I could hear you befo—" My ears twitched when a heard a quiet snap sound from my wrist. I looked down and gasped when I realized that Zora had attached a small, metal bracelet, similar to a thick hand cuff, to my right wrist. "What are you doing?"

The black haired woman smirked, her eyes betraying a darkness I had failed to notice before, and started to push me toward the force field. Her mouth opened in a sneer and she only stopped moving when my back was half an inch from the only thing keeping us inside the station.

"Zora," I whispered, trying to keep my voice level. I had hoped to distract her while I teleported away but, for some reason, neither of my powers were working. "Zora. What's going on?"

She smirked again, this one lifting her mouth up so high it looked like it might reach her ear. "What's it look like?" she asked me, her tone lower than normal. "I'm pushing you to your death just as you did to that alien."

"What? Why?"

I tried to kick her but she was gripping me too tightly. I managed to land one blow on her foot but she didn't even react. She was far superior to me in strength and resistance.

Zora looked me over, likely counting how much time she'd have before Di checked on us, then shrugged. "I suppose you have a right to know. A quick monologue shouldn't destroy my plan."

"And what's your plan?" Would she, a character who had never appeared in the show before, finally explain to me who she really was? Maybe this villain monologue would delay her long enough for Derek to check on me. He was still really paranoid, after all.

Zora took a deep breath, her eyes glazing over. "I was abused my entire life by my father and my step-father and my boyfriends, all three, and I've never been able to experience love of any kind from anyone. What did I do to deserve it? Absolutely nothing!" To emphasize it she leaned forward, her words reminding me of a snake's hiss.

"I used to tolerate it, to be kind, to figure that if I was sweet and good enough, eventually fate would give me someone nice. Someone sweet who would actually care about me instead of what I could do for him. But no. That. Never. Happened."

"Okay." Despite hanging on the brink of death I still felt pity for her. "Go on."

She sneered, insulted that I seemed to care. "Finally, I come here and meet the man of my dreams, the man I can already tell is my soul mate, the one I was born to love and marry and grow old with."

I furrow my brow. She's not talking about John Philips, is she?

"The only problem is, he's married."

Oh! She was talking about Derek? ...What?

"I've never asked for anything in my life. This is the first time I've ever, honestly wanted something all to myself." Her eyes started to well up with tears. "Is that so much to ask?"

"It is when he's married," I answered. I didn't mean to be snarky and annoy the woman trying to kill me but, as Derek's wife, I was very protective of him.

Predictably, it did annoy her and she shoved me a few millimeters closer to the force field. "You know," she hissed. "My mother was also a Valdis. She came from that other world too," she whispered, making my eyes go wide.

Was that the key to being a Valdis? Did you have to come from Earth to get the powers? Could there be even more worlds out there?...But, why did Polly get powers but Zora hadn't? Unless she was hiding them.

"There's apparently a fifty-fifty chance of Valdis offspring inheriting the gene. I was on the sad side of the fifty percent." It was as though she'd read my mind.

"My dad was a tad...over protective of my mother," Zora explained. "So he designed this. It kept her from using her powers and stopped those annoying nightmares she always had." She tapped the top of my bracelet with an angry glare. "After I killed him, I stole it. Always kind of figured I'd find a use for it."

"Zora, please. If you let me go I'll give you anything you want. I can find a way to make you happy. You just need love and care and I can provide that for you if you'll just—"

"I don't want you to help me. I don't care about you. I just care about Derek."

"He won't love you, Zora."

"He'll learn to. I can tell."

"You can't just force someone to love you."

"Why not?"

"Because..." Something about this felt odd. It seemed kind of strange that Zora would latch onto Derek so easily. She'd only known the guy for one day and while he was handsome, he wasn't the hottest guy in the world.

...That reminded me of something I'd always questioned when looking at Polly, my daughter. She had blonde hair like me. But, in the show, she had always had brown hair. I had figured it was because she took after Dark but that had been proved wrong. That meant Polly's mother needed to have dark hair.

Secondly, if what Zora said was true about Valdis, the original wife needed to either be a Valdis, which was unlikely, or the child of a Valdis. And Zora fit both those criteria...

My heart shattered. As I stared at her, this woman so broken apart by the world, my heart filled with fear and regret.

"You're the wife."

Her brow's furrowed. "What?"

"You were the wife." The one character the fans had never been able to meet. The one who had inspired Dark to destroy Manica. The one he had been madly in love with. "You're the wife!"

"Could you please shut up!?!" Zora yelled, on the brink of throwing me.

For the first time since this day had started I felt actual, honest to goodness fear. If I died here, the chances of Derek marrying her and loving her were high. He could move on without me! He might even forget everything we had promised to do!

"No!" I started to struggle, trying to kick her and bite her and yank my hands out of her grasp, all to no avail.

Zora smiled, likely happy that she'd inspired fear in me, even if she didn't know why. "Enjoy the afterlife, wife," she giggled before placing both palms on my chest and shoving me into space. I think she said something else afterwards but I couldn't hear her because the helmet I was wearing sealed to protect me from the oxygen-free air.

I didn't feel the force field pass through me. All I felt was panic. My heart was jumping up and down, my hands were shaking, my mouth was dry, my ears were ringing.

I was going to die!

Chapter 32

"Don't you think they should be back by now?" I asked Di, leaning back in the chair she'd provided. Both teams should have returned. What was keeping them?

My fears were about to dissipate when I heard the door open but the tremors in my heart didn't end because only Zora and my stupid boss were standing there. I thought he'd left.

"Where's Mary?" I asked, rising from the chair slowly. "Is she—"

Zora's eyes started to tear up, which only made me more afraid. Waving her gun at the ceiling, she walked toward me. "They killed her."

Huh?

My numb mind thought that over for a moment, trying to figure out if there was an alternate meaning of what she'd just said. Killed? Mary? Who was they?

Once the full realization struck me, the world started to spin. I felt ready to throw up and had to lean over the desk to keep from fainting.

"You're lying!" I whispered, my throat too dry to form the words fully. "That's impossible."

"Those three..." She pointed at the far door, her voice cracking from emotion. "They pushed her out into space. Said something about how she'd keep them from stealing the alien artifact. I tried to stop them but..." Her voice cracked once more and she had to look down, unable to continue speaking.

I couldn't believe it. Mary couldn't have died. I wouldn't have allowed it. "Is this true?" I asked, looking to John, the last man in Manica I'd ever want to ask.

The coward nodded slowly, his entire body shaking. "If it weren't for Zora we'd be dead too," he whispered, fiddling with the gun dangling from his hand.

"That..." It couldn't be real. I had to be dreaming. "But she's a Valdis. Why didn't she teleport?"

"They put some device on her," Zora answered, clenching her teeth in anger. "I should have stopped them. I shouldn't have run!"

My body suddenly snapped out of its stupor. I ignored Zora and ran to the computer, suddenly yelling for Di to bring up the security cameras. I needed to see this for myself. If this was true, which it totally wasn't, then I could still save her. There had to be a way!

"I detect a heat signature floating toward Manica," Di informed me as I brought up the footage. "I've dispatched a drone but it will fail to reach her in time."

"Do something!" I screamed at the top of my lungs, my nose starting to sting and making my eyes water. "She can't die!"

I was trying to come up with a plan B but as soon as I rewound the video and saw John shoot the camera, I turned on him with my teeth bared. His eyes were wide. He knew he'd been caught.

"You were in on this too?" I hissed, drawing my pistol from my belt and aiming it toward his heart. Actually, maybe I should aim at his head. He might not have a heart.

He stepped back, whimpering like a dog, but I didn't lower the barrel.

"Why?" I asked but already knew the answer. He wanted the alien artifact. They all did. They knew it would bring in more money than anything else in this world. They had killed my wife over it!

"Why did you bring him in here?" I yelled, turning my gun toward Zora. "Are you in on this too?"

The woman shook her head. "I couldn't care less about that ball of yours. I just wanted him here so he could prove I was telling the truth. Then I was planning to kill him."

True to her word, as soon as she finished speaking, she pulled out her own gun and shot him through his open, screaming mouth. She then sent a second bullet through his left eye as he fell to his knees and splatted on his bloody face. I didn't feel an ounce of regret as he fell.

Now I was at a cross roads. Trust Zora, who had no motive, or kill her and believe in Ace and the others.

"Di." I turned to the computer, my gun still trained on Zora. "Where are the others right now?"

Di studied the security cameras. "They were in the hangar bay. They are now on their way here. They should arrive in a few minutes."

"Derek," Zora pleaded, lowering her weapon. "I swear on my father's grave that I am telling you truth. I would never think of killing your wife. She was the sweetest woman I have ever known."

"But...Ace..."

"Jala was the one who orchestrated it and he is in love with her. Why wouldn't he work with her?"

"What?" I was so confused. I had to make a decision. I needed to choose. What should I do? What if they tried to kill me too?

My head was spinning. The floor was tipping back and forth as though I was on a cruiser. Back and forth. Back and forth. I could feel the back of my head burning. I could hear every breath I took. In and out. At times like this, when I felt something pressing on my heart, when I wanted to strangle someone, Mary had always managed to calm me down.

How was I supposed to control this rage if she wasn't here?

"Have you saved her?" I yelled at Di.

"It is too late, Derek. I am sorry. She has made contact with Manica's surface. At the speed she was falling, there was a...zero percent chance of survival."

I couldn't hear anything. More spinning. I was rotating now. The pressure was too much. I needed to scream or throw something or punch something until my hands bled and I could no longer hear the ringing in my head.

Then the door opened.

Perfect timing.

Jala was the first one to step inside, her expression one of anger until she spotted the blood covered body on the ground. After witnessing that and noticing the gun in my hand, her expression shifted into one of fear.

As soon as I saw her step inside, I turned the barrel of my on her. I wasn't taking any chances.

In the show, I had become the villain. It was Jala who made Ace betray me, who made him leave me on the moon by myself. In the show, she'd been the one to kill my daughter. In the show, she'd been the one who killed me. It was always Jala.

There was no question about it now. She had done it. She had killed my wife. She'd hurt me in another reality so why wouldn't she do it now? She and I were destined to be enemies forever. "Good" and evil. Head to head. More like evil and evil, really.

As I stood there with Zora at my side and John Philip's dead body lying at the tips of my boots, I made a decision.

I decided that I would spend the rest of my life hunting down these three heroes and killing them off one by one. I could kill them now, sure, but I would wait to murder them.

I'd let them escape. I'd let them think they'd won.

But I wouldn't let them live and I wouldn't let them steal the artifact. I would use it against them. I'd use the very thing they'd been after to kill them.

As my expression shifted to one I'm assuming was filled with rage, I felt Zora relax and take a step back from me, allowing me my vengeance without interference. Good. I wanted it that way. I didn't need help.

Jala continued to stare at me almost daring me to fire.

Challenge accepted.

I pulled the trigger.

The bullet tore through the flesh on her skinny arm and the impact sent her into the doorway where Maddox and Ace had been standing out of sight. She had barely risen from the cold floor, her blood soaking her clothes, when I cocked the gun and aimed it at her other arm.

"I would suggest that you run," I whispered, walking toward her slowly, deliberately. "Run away, hero. Run and hide so I can find you and tear your limbs off one at a time." And I would. Dark had done it before so why couldn't I?

"You're insane," Jala yelled at me, no longer caring why I was so mad. She spat in my direction before tearing down the hallway, screaming for Ace and Maddox to follow her.

"You were insane for killing my wife!" I called after them, shooting the ground beneath their feet to keep them going. "You thought you could steal from me? The man who hired you? The man who saved your lives? Betrayal must be in your blood because no matter what I do you still manage to take away everything I love!"

Now I understood why Dark had been so angry. He had seemed so irrational before, so bipolar, but now I could sympathize with him.

Mary had been my foundation. My pillar. My savior. And now that she was gone I had nothing to hold me up. I had relied too much on her through the years. Now nothing could fill that void.

As I'd watched the live footage of my wife floating toward her death, her body no more than a speck in the video, I had felt every inch of life drain from me. I was nothing more than a shell now. The remains of a man who had once been full of hope for the future was gone.

Now, I was the villain. Did I care? Not one bit.

As I walked back to the control room, shoving Zora out of the way so I could focus on the control panel, my shoulders began to shake from the sobs threatening to break free. I couldn't see the screen. My vision was a blur of black and blue. The metallic taste of blood was filling my nose and mouth. Maybe it was John's. Maybe it was mine. Was there even a difference anymore?

"Di," I whispered, throwing my gun across the room so I could use my hands to wipe the clear liquid off my face. "Now that John is dead, Hikarius needs a new leader. Send the news that he's been killed by a rogue alien and order all available employees to return to the station."

"Yes, sir."

"And...bring Polly here. I need to see her."

"Yes, sir. And her nanny?"

"...Fire her."

"Are you certain, sir?"

"You're not self-aware, Di! Just do what I tell you!"

"Yes, sir."

Chapter 33

The space station was getting farther away.

I could feel the air closing in on me. Were you even supposed to call it air?

Thank goodness I was still wearing my space suit, though it wouldn't do much good when I hit the world's surface. Why was the moon so close to Manica anyway? Wouldn't that create tsunamis or something? I'd never been big on science but it sounded like a logical question.

No matter how much I tried I couldn't get the bracelet off my wrist. It was thick and too tight to be wriggled out of. I hated it. Hated it!

Was I speeding up? It felt like I was.

Yup. Manica was even closer now.

Would it hurt when I hit the ground?

My heart rolled over itself. I didn't want to die. What would happen to Derek? What would happen to Polly? What would happen to me?

If I died here would I die in real life? Was this real life now?

Maybe this was all just a dream and when I landed I would wake up in my bed at home, still a hopeless teenager with no dreams. That would be preferable to this.

It was starting to get warm instead of cold now. I must have reached the atmosphere. Wonder why it wasn't burning me to a crisp. Maybe the atmosphere was different here compared to Earth. I didn't know. I'd never cared enough to look it up.

...You know, maybe my death would be for the best. I was never supposed to come here, after all.

Zora was supposed to marry Dark. She had been alone, afraid, desperate. Derek had been the one to love her, care for her, save her. She'd probably died happy.

Then I had stepped in. I had replaced her and taken away what little joy she might have enjoyed before dying. I had stolen her life.

In a way, I had been the villain.

I had saved Derek but destroyed Zora.

Yes. Maybe I deserved to die.

I slowly opened my eyes, which had been squeezed shut so I couldn't see the fast approaching world, and lost my breath. It was so close now. I could almost feel it.

I didn't want to die. I didn't care what I'd done, I just didn't want to die.

I don't want to die!

Derek!

I don't want to die!

Dark!!!

Ugh. I must have...fallen asleep. Where was I?

It felt like I was floating. Like I'd landed in a pile of clouds and they were wrapping around me like bubbles from a child's bathtub. It was so cold. So, so very cold.

And...

Everything burned. A searing pain bit at every part of my body, a pain that outdid the burns I'd gotten as a child when I touched the stove. It outdid the pain of childbirth. There was so much and it was so fast and everywhere and it hurt!

I wanted to scream. I wanted to thrash around and try to escape the awfulness that was my current existence but I couldn't even blink without using every ounce of my energy. I thought death was supposed to be warm and numb, not like this.

My brain was barely able to register a small, whirring noise above my head. The glass on my helmet had shattered and I think one of the shards was embedded in my cheek, not that I could tell since the pain wasn't focused on just one area.

The whirring came from behind me and I could see, out of the corner of my eye, a small familiar looking robot. My mind was so loud from the aches and pain that it took me more than one second to remember where I'd seen the metal thing but it finally registered that this was Odette's mini bot, Joe. I'd only remembered his name because it was the same as my brother's.

I wasn't sure what little Joe was doing but I didn't have time to find out because the corners of my eyes were turning an inky black and I fell into a restless sleep where the pain was just as bad and the nightmares were far worse than reality.

Chapter 34

"Mr. Hacket." The male voice rang from the speaker above my head and shook the floor underneath my chair. If he hadn't been so loud I might not have looked up from my computer screen with its distracting video feeds and top secret Hikarius documents. Ever since I'd become the new president, a title given to me after news of John Philip's death spread, I'd been given access to everything the company offered from hidden, experimental weapons to nuclear codes. I didn't plan to use them, though, since my alien artifact was ten times more powerful than anything they could offer.

Pushing my chair from the desk with my feet, I leaned back and angled my head toward the speaker. "What do you want?"

"Your daughter has arrived."

Finally! Something I wanted to hear.

As I marched toward the door my hands started to sweat and my throat became parched. I was racking my brain for a nice way to break the news to Polly because she didn't know what had happened here.

I'd merely told her she'd be allowed to live on the station with me from now on. She'd assumed I'd meant Mary would be here too.

When I unlocked the door I found Zora standing before me, a gun strapped to her leg and a black hat covering the top of her head. She shot me a smile, one I still didn't trust, before stepping aside and allowing me to see my child for the first time in months.

She was still short for an eleven year old and her baby face made her look eight, a fact that she hated. I had always encouraged her, though, telling her that her growth spurt would arrive any day now.

Seeing her blonde hair and bright eyes, which grew brighter as she smiled at me, sent my heart throbbing and, before I could stop them, tears started streaming down my cheeks. She looked so much like her mother. I couldn't stand it.

"Daddy? What's wrong?" Polly asked as she clasped one of my shaking hands between her small, warm ones. "Where's Mom?"

Her questions grew muffled as I pulled her into the longest hug I think I'd ever given. I couldn't let her see me cry. I was supposed to be the strong one. I wasn't supposed to be the one who fell apart from loneliness and sorrow.

I was pathetic.

A few of the passing employees, all of whom had arrived a few days ago from the company to help me with my work, stared at me judgingly and that was enough to snap me out of my sobs so I could glare at them.

The only employees whose presence I didn't mind were the soldiers I'd hired to help me hunt down my wife's murderers. They were standing on each side of my door, dressed in black armor and helmets that covered their faces. If I gave the order, they could kill anyone I wanted. That was why I liked them. That and they didn't flinch when I started throwing heavy objects around the room to distract myself from thoughts of Mary.

"Everything's gonna be okay," I told my daughter, still holding her close as we entered the room. "I'm going to make everything okay."

"Why? What's wrong?" The girl's eyes darting back and forth between mine in search of answers. I felt a shiver run down my back in reaction to her intense stare. She'd be able to tell if I was lying or not so there was no point in hiding it.

"Polly." I took a deep breath, sucking in air to keep my nose from stinging. "It's about your mother."

I had been trapped in the dark for so long. The pain had subsided quite suddenly a while ago but I hadn't woken up. I knew I was sleeping and had been for hours, years maybe, but I couldn't seem to tear myself out of this mass of black ooze. It wrapped around my brain, dulling my thoughts and senses.

That's why, despite how bright it was, I felt relief when my eyes opened and started to sting from the giant light shining on my face. It reminded me of the lights they'd used at the dentist when examining your teeth, only this one was far brighter. Plus, it had been dark for so long that my eyes couldn't handle the adjustment.

"This isn't a good time to wake up," a voice to my right informed me. The male voice grated on my ears and I wanted to slap whoever it was for interrupting the blissful silence.

As soon as I knew I wasn't alone, though, I started to realize that this person was doing something to me. I couldn't feel it, since my whole body was frozen stiff, but they were poking around inside my stomach with some sort of device, similar to a dentist using a pick to look at my teeth.

"W..." I wanted to ask "Who are you?" but couldn't muster the strength. "Why am I still alive?" would have been another excellent question but, as I said before, I was more useless than a rag doll.

"Just doing one of my annual checks," the man informed me, removing the metal prick he'd been poking me with and turning off the light. "To be honest I thought you were brain dead or something, what with you never waking up."

How long had I been asleep?

Once he turned off the light I finally managed to get a good look at this stranger. He was an older man, maybe in his sixties or seventies (I wasn't good at guessing one's age based on appearance alone) and had a wrinkled face. He had grey hair with a few white streaks running through it, which looked so good it was likely intentionally dyed, and his eyes were a similar color, a blue so light that they could have identified as grey.

Wrapped around his head was some sort of blue bandana, which looked quite comical, and his eyes were covered in thick glass, which was wrapped around his whole head with a brown strip of leather. Yes, he looked quite silly.

I wasn't sure if I wanted to trust this mad scientist look-alike but had no other choice. It wasn't like I could defend myself. Not with this stupid, metal bracelet around my wrist. I could still feel its cold bite.

"I suppose you'll want to know who I am and, since you can't speak, I'll just answer all the questions I would have had if I was in your position. Ahem." He cleared his throat and sat in a nearby, wooden chair, placing his hands in front of him like an attentive child. "No. I will not be giving you any alcohol."

I squinted at him, wishing I had the strength to scoff.

"Sorry. I'll be serious now." He giggled at his own sad attempt at humor. "My name is Alphenstine and you are lying in my home. I live in a tiny town, which you've probably never heard of, halfway up the Isabel mountains."

A mountain?

"Here I was, minding my own business and cleaning up a few of Odette's little robots when Joe here..." He pointed to Odette's little service bot who was sitting in the corner of the room.

Odette had closed down her bar a few years after I got married but I'd never bothered to ask where she'd sent her assistant bots. Now I knew.

"He rushed in and told me he'd found some girl trapped inside a pile of snow.

"So I followed him and sure enough, there it was. Tallest pile of snow I've ever seen in my life. It must have been three stories high. Took me half an hour to dig my way through. And just like Joe said," He shot Joe a thumbs up, "there you were smack dab in the middle wearing some kind of broken space suit. It was kind of freaky to see all the nearby snow covered in so much blood and even freakier to see your limbs all messed up but there's no need to worry. I've fixed them up and they've been healing really well."

So I'd landed in a conveniently placed pile of snow and that had been enough to save me a fall from space? I didn't buy it.

"I hate to break it to you, though. You won't be able to walk ever again."

I felt all color drain from my face.

"I couldn't find one part of your body that wasn't broken or mangled in some way. It's a miracle you survived at all. That's why I was so convinced you were stuck in a coma forever, seeing as how you were asleep for so long."

I opened my eyes as wide as they could go in the hopes that I could communicate my question. How long? How long had I been asleep?

Luckily, this guy wasn't as stupid as he acted. He knew what I was asking for. "You've been asleep for eleven months."

What?!?

I remembered how she'd looked when we'd learned about Polly.

Her face had gone completely pale, so much so that her skin had matched the color of her light blonde hair. Seeing her that way made me feel conflicted because what she'd just told me had given me the opposite reaction. I was thrilled.

"What's wrong?" I whispered, pulling my wife closer and running my finger across her cold cheeks. "Do you not want this?"

Mary shook her head. "I don't think I can be a mother, Derek. I...If she dies then I won't be able to stand it."

A knife played with my heart as I pulled her into my arms, pressing her cheek against my shoulder so she could cry without feeling embarrassed. What should I say? She didn't want this baby and I did. I wanted to raise children with her and grow old with her. I wasn't afraid of the "fate" that had been laid out for me because I knew we could change it.

"I love you," I whispered in her ear, making her nod slowly. "I will never let anything happen to you or our child, understand?"

My wife nodded again but pulled away, her reddening eyes boring into mine. "You have to promise me that no matter what happens to me you will not, under any circumstances, harm Polly."

"Of course I won't."

"You need to let her go to school and live a normal life and act like a kid." Her voice rose in desperation. "Please promise me that, Derek. Please." Her hands were roaming my face now, her eyes envisioning a future where she didn't exist.

She was about to say please again when I grabbed both of her hands and placed them against my heart, letting her feel the soft pounding within. "I would never do anything to hurt either of you," I told her but her face told me that I already had in another reality.

This was the memory that had repeated itself in my dreams ever since Polly had come to the station. As I sat in my cot, watching my daughter as she slept peacefully, tears created a path down my face.

Mary had been ready. She'd been expecting her death. She'd been preparing me and I'd been too stubborn to listen. Now I was alone, left with nothing but her words to haunt my nightmares.

Chapter 35

I had been slipping in and out of the darkness for months. The only time I ever woke was when the pain killers stopped working. Then I'd yell for the mad scientist and he would feed me some food and help me to the bathroom before he put me back to sleep. The pain was too much to stand for more than ten minutes so our meetings didn't last long before I fell unconscious again for a few more days.

Lucky for me, the more time my body had to heal, the longer my waking moments became. Once my bodily functions were met I'd start asking Alphenstine more questions about my survival and what was happening in Manica. He always helped me with the first question but never the second one. He always said current events didn't interest him.

He was apparently obsessed with the Valdis. Said that if he ever found one he'd experiment on it to find out its secrets. That was why I'd never explained how that snow mound had come to be.

You see, during my fall I had found that, although my powers had become incredibly limited, I hadn't lost all my gifts. I had used every ounce of strength to gather the snow together moments before I'd hit it. I'd also tried to use my telekinesis to slow my fall even more but it had only been enough to save my life, not to keep my body from getting flattened like a pancake.

My telekinesis was useless, though. Unless I got this bracelet off I wouldn't be able to use it and there was no way to remove the blasted thing.

I'd asked Alphenstine to get rid of it but he'd kept saying he might accidentally cut off my arm instead. The only part of me he didn't mind cutting off was my hair, which he continually shaved to keep out of the way. It was starting to grow out a little more now and I'd been taking care of it lately to keep it short so it didn't look too bad.

This was my life now. I had to sit by and wait for my body to heal the all-natural way with a tiny bit of help from my Valdis powers. No matter what I did, it still took too long.

Each time I woke up my head would rush through all the possible outcomes of Zora's actions. How was Derek doing? Was Polly okay? Had they moved on without me? Normally, that last thought would have seemed depressing but in my case it would have been good. Moving on meant Derek wouldn't turn into Dark.

All I could do was wait and have faith in my husband. I had to trust that he hadn't become the villain.

He couldn't have, right?

"Derek."

I turned away from my daughter, who was too distracted by Di to pay attention to me anyway, and watched as Zora entered my office, which had formerly been the control room. It felt like I'd been seeing a lot of her lately.

"Derek, can I speak to you in private?" she asked me, casting a glance at my distracted daughter. "I have matters to discuss with you."

"I'll be right back, Polly," I told the preteen who barely looked away from Di's face long enough to nod.

Satisfied, I joined Zora outside the room and shut the door, motioning for the guards to walk away and give us a moment alone. "What is it? Have they found Jala yet?"

Zora shook her head. "That's what I'm here to talk about."

I waited.

"I think it's time you stopped hunting them."

"What? That's ridiculous. They murdered my wife."

"But you could be spending the time you've spent hunting them doing more productive things. What about those weapons we talked about making a few months ago? What about taking over Manica and bringing world peace? You're wasting the potential that alien artifact has given you."

"Yeah, well, your vision of world peace is different from mine. I'm not the dictator type."

"Then give me the power. I am more than capable of running the country on my own."

"Sure," I drawled sarcastically. "Letting one person rule alone is definitely going to work."

"What if your wife was the one asking? Then would you do it?"

"Don't bring her into this," I growled.

The rawness in my voice made her steel expression soften and she rested a hand on my arm, making me flinch. "I'm worried about you Derek. This obsession isn't good for you. You need to forget about Mary and move on to do—"

"Forget my wife? What's wrong with you?" I yelled before glancing down the halls to make sure no one had heard me.

Zora smiled like a caring mother. "I didn't mean forget. I just meant that you need to move on and the best way to get over a lost love is to replace it with another. I can do that for you, Derek."

What was she thinking? "No one will be able to replace my wife."

"You're right." She sighed, placing her hands on her hips. "I'm using all the wrong words today. I'm saying that I care about your well-being, Derek, and I just want to ensure that you're okay physically and mentally."

"I'm fine!"

"And what about Polly?" she suddenly asked loudly. It was strange to have her stand up to me like this. It reminded me of when Mary used to do it, though Zora was more authoritative.

"What about her?"

"Polly needs a mother in her life."

"She has me."

"She has a father who cares more about her mother's killers than her. She needs a woman in her life, Derek, and I can do that. I hate to see you two wasting away."

Derek, Derek, Derek. Why did she keep saying it like that? I hated it! "Stop calling me that!" I suddenly yelled, punching the wall so I wouldn't end up hurting her instead. "Don't call my name!"

"What?" Zora backed away, her lips pursed in confusion. "I'm sorry. I didn't know it offended you. I ... what should I call you?"

My mind flashed back to the show. What had my name been in that? It started with a D. I wanted to remember it. I needed that name. I needed to use it so I'd stop remembering Mary and everything associated with her. If people called me by a different name then I'd stop hearing Mary's voice anytime they said it.

"Call me Dark," I whispered, not caring how lame the title was. It was the one I'd been given and the one I wanted. Something about it felt right. Natural. "Don't ever call me Derek again, understood?"

She nodded hesitantly, fear entering her eyes for the first time. Good. I liked it that way.

Chapter 36

"Maddox!" Now, to find that small town he'd mentioned.

I frowned, pulling myself out of my daydream. Jala was calling me. What did she want?

Allowing my eyes to adjust to the darkness of the basement we'd spent the last three days in, I turned toward the woman. Ace was seated beside her, his head tipped sideways in sleep and his hand encircling hers.

Jala studied me for a moment, her eyes likely trying to see through my helmet, before she sighed and gestured toward the backpack at her feet. "You can eat now," she told me, knowing I never ate in front of others. "Do it before he wakes up."

I nodded, grabbed the bag, and stalked into the farthest corner where I could be alone. After glancing back at the pair one last time to make sure they weren't watching, which was unlikely since they were now sleeping on each other's shoulders, I hesitantly pulled off my helmet and began tearing into the loafs of bread Jala had provided.

I was nearly finished when I heard a voice coming from within my helmet. Thinking it was malfunctioning, I slipped it back on and started fiddling with the buttons on the outside, unsure what was wrong.

"H...hello?"

I frowned again. A voice? There was a female's voice echoing over the radio on what was supposed to be a secure channel. Unless Jala was messing with me, there was cause for alarm.

Moments before I disabled the connection, the woman spoke again.

"Hello? Maddox? Anyone?"

I shouldn't have answered. I should have disabled my radio until I knew it was secure. I considered doing so but finally decided that there was nothing to lose by answering. After all, what else could this world possibly take from me?

"Yes. Who is this?" I asked.

The voice flooded with relief. "Thank goodness. I thought I'd never find you."

"Who is this?"

Hesitation. "...It's Polly."

Derek and Mary's daughter?

"I've been really lonely lately so Di gave me your number."

This wasn't exactly a number but that didn't matter. How had Di known where to contact me? "What do you want?"

Another long pause filled with shallow breaths. "I was hoping we could be friends."

"I don't have friends."

"That's fine." She countered quickly. "We can become friends."

"How would your friendship benefit me?"

She took a moment to come up with an answer. "I could keep you updated on my father's doings. That way he'd never be able to catch you."

That sounded useful. "And all I need to do is talk to you?"

"Yup."

Her childish voice didn't match the gift she was offering. I hesitated, weighing the pros and cons of forming such a bond, then shrugged. "Very well."

Another sigh of relief. How hard up was she for friends? It's not like she was locked away from the world or anything. "I have one final question."

"Yeah?"

"Why me?"

"...No real reason."

Good enough for me.

"I've told you a thousand times, Mary." Alphenstine groaned dramatically and went back to fiddling with Joe's circuits. The sweet little robot had been acting up lately and it had all the other bots nervous. "I don't like contacting the outside world. When you're well enough you can walk down to the town and ask them to contact your family but until then you will stay here. I am not escorting you down there."

This was the tenth time we'd had this conversation. I had been trapped on top of this mountain for 35 months now and this hermit's stubbornness had deterred me from contacting Derek. The only other person I'd seen during that time had been a kind lady who stopped by once, three months ago. She'd left before I could ask her for help, though.

"This is ridiculous," I growled, feeling heat rise in my chest. "I never should have stayed here in the first place. If you'd taken me to a real hospital I could have healed in three months instead of three years."

"Be thankful I've taken you in at all!" he answered before handing me a glass of water to calm me down.

I accepted the glass but didn't drink it, frowning at my scarred reflection. My body was almost fully healed, though it was painful to get around and I always needed a crutch to hold me up. My habit of sleeping for days at a time had ended months ago but I was still drowsy all the time. It was starting to seem a bit suspicious.

"Drink your water," Alphenstine told me, shutting Joe's back and letting him scooter off to do his own thing. "You need to stay hydrated."

"I'll go down to the town on my own," I whispered, looking up from the clear liquid.

The man frowned, his googly eyes squinting. "We've been over this. You would collapse half way down and then you'd freeze to death. It's much safer here."

"I can't heal if I stay here," I stated. "Not fully."

"That's because you haven't been resting enough."

"I've been resting for years. I have a family, Al, and they could be in trouble without me!"

He squinted. "So, you would ignore my hospitality and run off?"

I sighed, feeling guilty. "I've taken advantage of your kindness long enough. Now I need to—"

"No."

"...What?"

The small man got up from his seat, picked up one of his sharp metal tools, and pointed it at me. "You're not leaving."

"What are you talking about?" My heart started to pound.

"For three years I've been studying you, dedicating all my time to caring for you, and you will not just walk away before my research is complete."

I rose, using the edge of my chair to support me before slowly edging toward the door. "You knew I was a Valdis?"

"Do I look stupid to you? Of course I knew! Why else would I take care of a whiney child like you? I would have left you in that snow mound to die if I hadn't known."

All these years I hadn't figured it out. I'd been too tired and depressed to realize I was being used. That must have been why he left the bracelet on, too. He had known it was holding me back, keeping me from escaping.

"Now, drink your water and go to sleep." He pressed the tip of the tool against my chest and nodded toward the bed I'd spent so many hours in, wasting away.

Without my powers I was scared. I was afraid of this little man. How pathetic. "Did you intentionally keep my injuries from healing?" I questioned, still unsure of how to escape.

"Stop asking questions! Just drink your water!"

"No, I'm not drinking your drugged water!"

"Do you want me to break your bones all over again?"

I'd had enough. Cringing as the muscles in my arms ached, I lifted the table between us and threw it at the man, knocking him against the wall and making him drop his weapon. I then grabbed the fallen tool and dug it into his shoulder, forcing blood to ooze and dribble down his arm.

"Joe!" I yelled before pulling the tip of the tool he'd used on me so many times out of his flesh and pointing it at his throat. "Open the door for me!"

Joe complied, using all the strength he had in his little body to swing the wooden door open, allowing the cold air to rush into the small cabin. Out of all the robots, he was the only one I had ever known personally. Earlier, the other ones had had their insides ripped out by the scientist and I'd been the one to defend Joe and save him from getting dismembered. Now, he was my only ally.

My ears started to ring as I wondered whether or not I should kill this man. On one hand, he had saved my life. On the other, he had imprisoned me for three years and kept me from my family.

After much deliberation I took the middle ground and tied him up. He'd find a way to get free somehow but this would give me enough time to keep him off my tail. Then, just to ensure my safety, I hit him over the head with a chair to knock him unconscious before rushing out the door with Joe on my heels.

Chapter 37

The town was visible from the cabin but there was a lot of steep snow covered terrain to cover between it and me. Joe wasn't built to travel through snow and my pathetic body was sluggish and numb. Alphenstine was probably right. I might freeze to death before we could reach our destination.   me.

"We can do it," Joe told me optimistically with the high pitched, child-like voice box the scientist had given him. "Do not stop."

"I won't," I whispered, hissing in pain as my legs started to ache. My lack of exercise from all the sleep was probably the most dangerous thing I had ever done. Now my pale, muscle free body could barely hold itself up.

The snow started to pile on top of my boots, a pair I'd swiped on my way out the door, and it was soaking my legs. To make matters worse, it was especially windy today and the air insisted on attacking every unprotected part of my body.

It took a couple hours to cross the area, a trek that normally should have taken twenty minutes, but I finally made it.

The "town" was no more than five houses and one general store. The buildings were small and made of wood, similar to the scientist's home, and their roofs were covered in thick layers of snow.

Joe went ahead of me and knocked on the first door he could find, sounding an alarm just in case the owner was sleeping. After a few moments, the door opened and a woman stepped out with a bat in her hand. It was the one who had stopped by to visit that one time.

I was guessing from the tight bun and hardened expression on her face that she had either been a soldier or went through some rough times in her life. The expression didn't change when she spotted me and lowered the bat, stepping over Joe so she could help me stand.

"So the old guy finally let you out?" she asked, leading me inside her sparse home where a fire was burning.

"No. I tied him up," I answered, collapsing on the nearest chair and leaning over to catch my breath.

"Oh. I'd always assumed you were his daughter." A look crossed her face that told me she had considered otherwise but obviously hadn't cared enough to look into it. "He didn't do anything to you, did he?"

I scoffed, feeling a tad annoyed at her for not helping me that one time. "Just took away three years of my life. Do you have a telephone?" I didn't want to discuss the past anymore and needed to get straight to the point.

The woman shook her head. "There aren't any lines that run this far up the mountain."

Of course. It could never be that easy.

"I would take you down myself," the woman continued, sounding genuinely concerned, "But the Hikarius raids have me nervous about going back to the city. I've heard about people dying down there and wouldn't want you to end up like my brother did."

"Raids? What raids?" That felt a bit too familiar for my liking.

"Oh. Right. You've been detached from society for a while. Hikarius has been hunting down a group of dangerous mercenaries and have been raiding every nearby town in the hopes that they'll find them."

That sounded a lot like Dark's hunt for Jala, Maddox, and Ace in the books.

"I used to think they were trying to look out for us but, in the past couple of months, they've started to get desperate, I think. They've been arresting and even killing people who they think are even remotely related to these criminals. They locked up my brother for three weeks before they released him. He'd never even heard of these mercenaries."

She kept clenching and unclenching her fists as she spoke, turning her knuckles white with each movement. "If they don't find them soon, Hikarius might get worse. I've considered joining them multiple times just to make them stop hurting people."

"Who is the leader of Hikarius?" I asked, hoping she'd say someone else was doing this. A name other than the one I dreaded.

"Hacket," she said, gritting her teeth. "I've heard he's insane."

"Why is he hunting these...mercenaries?"

"They said it was because they were criminals but...my brother told me differently. He said that when he was locked up he got to meet Hacket personally and learned the real reason for the raids."

"And?"

"He's hunting them because they murdered his wife."

My eyes went wide. What? Not because they'd betrayed him?

The woman rose when she saw how pale and shaky I'd become. "Hey, are you okay?" she asked, gripping my clammy hands and looking into my eyes. "What's the matter?"

"You need to take this off!" I yelled, shoving the thick bracelet in her face. "If you take it off I can stop Hacket! Please get it off me!" I hated it. I hated it!

"Okay, okay." She released me, probably thinking I had lost it, and ran a hand over it to see how much work it would take to remove. It would take more than a wire cutter to remove. "Just calm down."

"I can't. I have to tell him that I'm okay. I threw away my life on earth for him and now he's gone down the same path despite everything we did. I need to save him before he dies." Some of the scientist's drugs must have still been in me because I still felt sick. I had to keep talking or else I'd fall unconscious again. I had to tell her what I was.

"Don't worry. I'll help you. Just take a deep breath and I'll find a way to get this shackle off."

"I'm Hacket's dead wife," I whispered, pulling her toward me. "I am Derek Hacket's wife."

"What?"

No sooner had I said the words that a desperate scream rang outside the building, making me jump out of my seat and look toward the door. Was it Alphenstine? Had he already found me?

The kind woman glanced over her shoulder, swore, then hauled me into her arms like I was a child. She kicked open the door to her closet and sat me inside, covering me with some clothes so I'd be hidden. She was about to lock the door but Joe managed to slip in and hide with me before she did so, which made me slightly less afraid.

"Do not come out until I give the okay," she ordered before closing the door, leaving me to shake and shiver from my exhausted body. I wanted to help her but with the bracelet on I could do nothing.

"We will be fine," Joe told me as the woman ran outside and shut the door behind her. "Do not worry."

"Of course I'm worried," I hissed, my breath quick and panicked. She didn't believe me. What if something happened to her?

I tried to reach the doorknob but my body refused and I could do nothing but collapse and listen to what happened outside.

Chapter 38

This town sure was tiny. Even I doubted the trio would be hiding here but we had to check everywhere. "I never should have let them escape," I muttered as I watched my men drag the citizens out of their homes and place them in the center of the town.

Only ten people. Two of them children. Wait. Eleven. One woman had just exited the farthest house. She had a bat in her hand. That was cute...and stupid.

I nodded toward her and one of my armored men grabbed her, dragging her down with the others. The bat was snapped in half before she was even on her knees.

Hmm. She looked like the type to hide fugitives so I'd check her house first.

As I stalked toward the front door I patted the back of my long black and red jacket to ensure that my gun was still on me. I was about to yank the door open when she yelled.

"Hacket!"

"What?" I turned toward her with a smirk, glad something interesting was happening today. "Can I help you?"

"If you're looking for criminals," she started, rising slowly with her hands above her head, "then I want to help. My father was part of the military and trained me. I could be a valuable asset."

This was more fascinating than her house. "Interesting propositio n...But how can I know you won't betray me? How do I know you're not secretly with the mercenaries?"

"Because I'm not a criminal."

"So you're a hero. Is that it?"

She hesitated, then nodded. "In a sense, maybe."

My right eye twitched. A hero, huh? That was what Jala had called herself in the show. "Tell me." I started toward her. "Would you be willing to do anything for me?"

She frowned in confusion as I pulled out my gun and placed it in her hand.

"Would you be willing..." I then aimed the barrel at my throat and looked her in the eyes. "...to kill me?"

"What?" Her eyes shot to her house, then to the children sitting behind her. "I couldn't without a reason..."

"I wouldn't always give you a reason," I answered, knowing she wouldn't do it. She wasn't the kind of soldier I was looking for. I didn't want heroes. I wanted anti-heroes, people like me who did what was wrong to do what was right.

She kept her fingers on the gun but didn't pull the trigger. "I won't kill for no reason. My moral compass doesn't aim that way."

"Fine." I licked my lips and nodded. "Okay, let's say that I raided every town in Manica just to find three people."

She frowned. She knew it was true.

"Let's say I imprisoned some of them because of my paranoia that they were working with the mercenaries."

She still refused to fire.

I smirked. "Let's say that I killed some of them...Let's say that my girlfriend and I killed a lot of them...Let's say that I'm going to kill everyone in this town just to lure the 'heroes' out."

"You wouldn't."

"Why wouldn't I?" I gave her the brightest smile I could, the one Zora told me made me look like a ladies' man, and waited.

I could tell that she was considering it. She even wrapped her finger around the trigger but, after glancing at the kids once more, she lowered the weapon and stepped back. She hadn't believed me.

I chuckled and grabbed the gun, shoved her back onto the snowy ground and walking away. Pathetic.

"Jala!" I yelled, marching between the houses. "If you come out now I'll let these people live!" If she was here then she'd come out to save these people. If she wasn't here then...false alarm.

"There isn't any 'Jala' here," the woman answered before receiving a blow to the head from one of my soldiers. A normal person would have backed down but she rose and punched him in the face, making him fall in the snow before the others could stop her. She had just grabbed his gun and was about to shoot him when the other soldiers disarmed her, shoving her onto her stomach.

I approached the fearless chick and frowned, watching her struggle like a child. "This is what I don't understand about you heroes," I told her, kicking the gun away from her as they tied her up. "You're willing to kill my henchmen but when you have the opportunity to kill their boss, the man who ordered them to perform all these dastardly deeds in the first place, you let me live. Why? Because I'm unarmed. Because of your misplaced sense of morality, you refuse to destroy the root of a problem."

She spat in my direction. "Your wife's lucky that she doesn't have to see you like this," she hissed before coughing up blood.

My heart lurched at her words and I pointed my gun at her head, feeling the pressure return to my head. "When I go on my next killing spree," I whispered, placing my finger on the trigger. "And I'm holding a gun to my next victim's head, I'll be sure to tell them the story of how you refused to kill me."

Her blood spattered all over my face when I pulled the trigger and the kids started to scream as soon as she lost a chunk of her head but their cries didn't make me feel guilty. On the contrary, their high pitched voices were grating on my ears. It was making my headaches worse.

I tossed the gun aside and headed back down the mountain, pressing my palm to the back of my head. "Kill them," I ordered. "All of them."

I could hear more screaming as I left. I even thought I heard one person scream my real name, but I ignored it. That woman had been asking for it. That's what "heroes" like her deserved.

Chapter 39

J oe was the best robot ever created.

After we spent two torturous days climbing down the mountain with only one bottle of water and a box of crackers, he informed me that the city at the base of the mountain was where Odette lived and he knew how to get there.

I found myself gaining more strength the closer we got to her house. It was a tiny building, probably with no more than two rooms, and had walls the color of cherries. I shouldn't have been surprised by the design choice.

She must have been sleeping because it took six rings for her to answer the door, dressed in white shorts and a red tank top. Even though she didn't look that different without makeup, seeing her face did give me start for a moment.

The middle aged woman looked at me once, then twice. Then she rubbed her eyes before dropping her jaw. "Mary, is that really you?"

I nodded, so relieved to see a familiar face. "Odette, you need to help me."

"Of course! Get in here!" She hurried Joe and me inside before checking both sides of the street to make sure no one had followed us. It wasn't until she shut the door and sat me down in the kitchen that she started talking.

"It's been three years! Where have you been? Everyone thinks you're dead!"

Now that I was in a safe place, my mind had settled down and I could tell the whole story without stuttering. As I related the whole tale to her, she started piling snacks on top the counter for me, probably in reaction to my substantial weight loss. I was nothing but pale skin and bones now.

"That's awful."

"Yeah." I completely agreed.

"No. I don't think you know how awful it is. Because of your death, Jala and Maddox and Ace are fugitives. Derek's been killing people to find them and Zora's been even worse."

I knew about the first part but hadn't heard anything about Zora.

"At least Derek is focused on finding these three and only kills if he's suspicious. When Zora goes out with the raiders she'll burn entire towns to the ground. She's got some kind of intense hatred for humanity. It's insane."

"What about Polly?"

"Hmm? I haven't heard much about her."

Then she's probably being used as a battery for the alien artifact and spaceship just like in the comics. That meant she was dependent on the artifact now and, if Zora decided to disconnect her, she would die.

"I need to save Polly and Derek. You need to help me get this off so I can find them." I held up the shackle.

Odette stared at it, then sighed, which was discouraging. "I can't do that," she told me, shaking her head without even bothering to ask what it was for. "...But I know someone who can."

"Who?"

The woman walked around the counter, stood next to me, then slammed her feet on the floor multiple times. Confused, I furrowed my brow for a moment until the carpet next to us lifted and revealed a trap door. Out of the secret door stepped Ace, followed by his two other partners in crime.

As soon as Ace saw me his eyes went wide, Jala wasn't affected, and Maddox was impossible to read. He was still dressed in the same outfit he'd been wearing three years ago.

"Maddox can get it off," Odette told me as the trio surrounded me. They didn't even bother asking how I was still alive. All they cared about was if I'd be able to stop Derek or, as he'd apparently been calling himself, Dark.

My heart was beating wildly as Maddox brought one of his special torches to my hand. The scientist's words about cutting off my arm still had me nervous and I found it hard to calm down as the helmeted man started melting away the thick metal.

I didn't feel anything until the concentrated flames were a millimeter from my flesh. Then, the searing pain was replaced by a feeling of light. As the shackle finally fell, I felt as though I'd lost twenty pounds. I also felt my body start to readjust to my old powers and my wounded body.

All four of my friends backed up when they saw what was happening to me. As I gripped my stomach and collapsed to my knees, my skin turned as white as the aliens' had been. Veins popped out on every part of my body and my eyes bulged as I gasped for air.

I could feel the blood rushing through my veins at the speed of light. My limbs were readjusting themselves, rubbing their bones together as they undid the damage Alphenstine had made. My muscles rippled and, with them, the pain increased, sending my brain spinning in circles.

Finally, the screams reached a limit and the pain completely disappeared, leaving my body completely whole and healthy, although I was still too thin from lack of food.

As I rose from the carpet, sighing loudly, I smiled evilly. I was healed. My powers were back and had fixed me. Being healthy never felt good unless you'd been really sick for a long time. Only then could you appreciate it. I'd never felt so good in my life.

As I lifted an apple into the air with my mind and took a bite, Odette smiled deviously.

"We've been hiding for years," she told me. "But now that you're here, we can become the hunters."

Hearing that made me nervous. Not only was her line super lame and cliché, but in the stories they had spent three months trying to reach the Hikarius station and it had taken a whole week to fight their way to Polly so they could kill her and lure Dark out. Then they'd killed him and gone off to participate in other, less interesting adventures. The popularity had started to dwindle after Dark died.

How would I save Polly? When we found her inside that box, controlling the ship and acting dependent on the artifact, would I be able to rescue her? Or would she be so desperate for death that she'd kill herself?

The thought of it made me want to vomit. I considered telling the others what to expect but thought better of it. Derek had known what had happened and look where that got him.

Jala was just beginning to discuss a plan of attack when Maddox lowered his head, pressed a finger to the side of his helmet, and nodded. "We've been discovered," he informed us, motioning to the front door before climbing back inside the floor and throwing weapons out for us to grab.

As though they'd done this a thousand times, the group leapt into action, arming themselves and barricading the doors. Meanwhile, I walked toward the nearest window and peered through the glass, trying to see who it was. Had Derek been the one to come?

My heart dropped into my knees when I saw Zora standing outside, a devilish grin on her face and a small army of soldiers at her side. She was the last person I wanted to see today.

Chapter 40

I was itching to burn this cherry house down. As my men knocked down the door and charged inside, guns at the ready, I rolled back and forth on my heels. My excitement must have been obvious because the soldier off to my left, the only one who hadn't gone inside with the others, kept glancing at me.

After I realized that I was being watched I stopped moving and glared at the soldier. "Why aren't you in there with them?" I asked, gesturing toward the men as they cleared the building.

The soldier glanced at the red house, then back at me. His entire body was hidden by a long, black cloak and his face covered by a silver mask that wrapped around his mouth like worms on a wet sidewalk. "I was giving you the honors."

I groaned, all joy gone. I hated this soldier most of all. If he wasn't so good at his job I definitely would have killed him long ago. I never should have suggested he join me on my hunt. "Just shut up and do your job."

The person chuckled, then headed into the house without a weapon. After checking all the rooms, they came back out to deliver a report. "They're gone."

My insides boiled. "What?!?"

The soldier shrugged. "I don't know how they escaped so quickly."

Neither did I. We had seen one of them through the window moments before breaking in. We should have seen them exit through a back door or window so where had they gone? Enraged, I kicked a nearby wall. "You didn't warn them beforehand, did you?" I hissed.

"Now why would I do that?" the man asked mockingly.

I shrugged, looking away. "I don't know. Just seems like something you'd do."

While the soldier laughed, I screamed inwardly. I'd need to report to Dark that I had failed to capture them. This had been my last chance to kill them and finally gain his trust. Now he'd probably hate me even more.

"I'm glad you're on our side," Jala told me with a genuine smile. "Thanks for saving us back there. Wish I could teleport."

I shrugged shyly as she and Ace sat next to me. We were resting on top of a small hill overlooking the city. The world didn't look so bad from up here. I almost forgot we were fugitives.

"This isn't the time to admire the scenery," Odette said, standing with her hands on her hips like a stern mother. "I haven't used a gun since I was in my twenties but I'm willing to make an exception for this so let's get a move on before Zora finds our hidden ship too."

The reason she'd owned the bar in the first place was to buy a space ship to get somewhere. She'd never specified where, though. Once she'd saved up enough, she'd sold the establishment. It felt oddly convenient that she had a ship just when we needed it, though.

"Fine with me." I glanced at Maddox, who was staring intently at Joe as he spun around his legs.

"You ready, Maddox?" Jala asked him, drawing him out of his silent conversation with Joe. The helmeted man nodded and picked up the service bot, planning to take it to the moon with them.

"Okay." Jala turned toward me, her eyes lit up in anticipation of revenge. "We're counting on you, Mary. Just don't get mad if we murder your psycho husband."

I hesitated to take her outstretched hand. "...Then don't get mad if I kill you afterwards."

The main character giggled like a villain, shrugging. "Fair enough."

Chapter 41

The pair of soldiers patrolling the halls looked identical in their red and black armored suits but on the inside, they couldn't be more different.

"I'm telling you," the first guy said enthusiastically, waving his gun back and forth. "If you just give Hareon music a chance you'll come to love it. The idols are talented and the music is great—"

"But they don't speak Manican," the other defended angrily, determined to stand his ground. "Plus, the music is weird."

"No weirder than Manican music."

"Manican music is normal. Hareon is not. It's so...dramatic."

"You're dramatic!" he countered, a comeback he'd probably spent months preparing. "And you're a hypocrite. You listen to 'Classy Man' and that's a Hareon song."

"But "Classy Man' has Manican words in it."

"But..." The soldier shook in frustration. "All Hareon songs have Manican words in them!"

Before the stubborn soldier could respond, both of them were knocked off their feet and dragged into a nearby closet where we were waiting. Jala knocked the anti-Hareon one out immediately but didn't with the other one, the butt of her gun poised to smack his head.

He stared back at her, breathing heavily. He wasn't sure why she was hesitating but it was making him even more nervous.

Jala waited a few more seconds, studying him curiously, before she lowered her gun and told Ace to tie him up. After he had done that, she leaned toward the frightened guard.

"Keep up the good work," she whispered with a smile before all five of us, plus the robot Joe, leapt out of the closet and shut the door behind us, leaving it unlocked so the two could eventually get out.

I shot Ace a questioning look as we ran, trying to figure out why Jala had left the second guy alone. Ace was the only one who would know the answer since he and Jala had been dating for so long.

"She's a fan of Hareon music too," he whispered with a chuckle before adjusting the gun in his hands and focusing on our mission. "She plays it constantly when we're alone." He sounded so defeated that I couldn't help but laugh.

We kept running through the station, ducking into small rooms whenever guards walked past, but we were still no closer to finding Derek's office. Everything looked so different and it felt more like a maze than anything.

"I wish they'd put a map on the walls or something," Odette commented as she peeked around a corner. "I've never been good with directions."

I was just starting to believe we were going in circles when a small, soulless voice echoed through our earpieces, using a channel that was supposed to be private.

"Have you come to kill him?" the female voice whispered, her tone hollow and echoey, as though whoever it was had been trapped inside a small room. She sounded so sad. So lonely. She sounded like...

"Is that Polly?" I whispered, glancing at Odette. The woman shrugged before pulling us into another room, watching our backs so we could talk to the mysterious voice.

"Who is this?" Jala asked, not ruling out the possibility that it was a trap. I was the one who didn't agree. I knew this voice. It was Polly. The same Polly I had seen on the show.

"It doesn't matter who I am," the girl whispered. "All that matters is that I help you find Dark."

"And how exactly do you plan to do that?" the leader asked mockingly.

"I control everything in this ship. I know where you are and I know that you won't be able to reach Dark without my help."

"Try me," Jala challenged.

"Jala!" I placed a hand on her shoulder and shook my head. "Trust her. She knows what she's talking about." Polly was the one who powered the entire station and kept it from crashing into the moon, with the help of the little alien sphere, of course.

Jala shot me a questioning look but didn't talk back. "...Fine. Tell us what you know?"

"Dark's office is guarded by the strongest guards and thickest doors in the entire station. He's the only one who lets anyone in or out. If you want to reach him, you need to lure him out."

"And how do we do that?" Ace asked.

"After he kills you he plans to use the moon's power source to dominate Manica. If you threaten the power source, he'll send men to defend it but if you destroy it, he'll be angry enough to come on his own."

"That stupid ball we found on the moon?" Jala asked, gritting her teeth. "That thing has been nothing but trouble ever since we found it."

"Where is the artifact?" Ace questioned, growing concerned about their situation.

"It's with me."

My heart started to race. This was exactly what had happened last time.

"I need you to find me, destroy the artifact, and kill Dark so I can be free to do whatever I please. I'm tired of working for him. He's too depressed to take care of now."

"But we won't need to hurt you in order to destroy it, right?" I asked desperately.

There was a moment of hesitation, then came a quick, "No."

"Okay." I sighed, feeling air rush out of my chest. "Thank goodness." Things had changed. She wasn't reliant on the stone in this reality. That took a load off my mind.

"I'll give you directions," the voice continued, "But you need to come right now!"

I raised an eyebrow. She really hated Derek...Dark now, just like in the show. He must have locked her up against her will.

"What's the rush?" Jala asked, glancing at Odette who was still guarding the closet door.

"Zora and her soldiers just arrived," the mysterious helper explained quickly. "And they know you're here. You need to hurry."

"You don't need to tell me twice," I whispered and opened the door.

Chapter 42

I would have described the boring halls of the station but there wasn't much to describe. The white and blue halls were empty other than the occasional security cameras and blank television screens. The only soldiers we encountered were easy to avoid and those who weren't were quickly escorted to the closets. The glass case was empty. Polly wasn't here.

Despite knowing that the climax of the story was almost upon us, I wasn't feeling especially nervous or excited. Trudging through these uninteresting halls wasn't doing much for me. Maybe spending three years asleep had taken the thrill out of me.

It didn't really strike me that we were still being hunted until we almost literally ran into Zora and her men. As soon as we spotted each other we immediately froze and took a defensive stance.

"Oh." Zora's face lit up and she stalked toward us, her heels clicking against the shiny floor and her lips curling upwards. "What a coincidence. How ironic that we would meet on today of all days."

Jala frowned and matched her stare, pistol in hand. "And why is that?"

"We decided to stop hunting you this morning," Zora informed us in a giggly voice. "Yet here you are, ready to surrender."

"Well, if you're not hunting us then I suppose we'll just be on our way." Jala answered.

"I said I stopped hunting you, not that I stopped wanting to kill you!"

Ace aimed his machine gun at the evil woman's head. "Touch a hair on her head and I'll riddle you with bullets."

Zora snickered. "Aww. Is she your girlfriend now?"

Ace clenched his teeth but didn't answer. His finger was lingering over the trigger and the only reason he hadn't fired was because he didn't want to be at the mercy of the rest of the soldiers behind her.

"And who are you?" Zora asked, finally drawing her attention to Odette and I. She was having fun messing with us. "I don't think I've seen you two before."

Odette shrugged nonchalantly. "Nobody important. And who are you, other than the woman who killed Dark's wife, of course."

Zora's face reddened at that and the hooded soldier behind her finally stepped forward, reaching into the folds of her cloak for a weapon.

"Who told you that?" Zora hissed at the older woman, pursing her lips.

"Enough." Jala pulled a shotgun off the back of her left leg, pressed it against Zora's chest, and fired with a sneer.

I immediately looked away, the shot echoing in my ears and my skin anticipating the splash of blood it would create. One second passed. Two. Nothing. We were still dry.

I turned back and my eyes went wide. Zora was still standing before us, perfectly healthy.

After a moment, my eyes were drawn to a slight shimmer hovering in front of Zora and I realized what had happened. Some kind of clear shield had wrapped around her body and the shards of Jala's bullets were lying at her feet.

Jala turned to me, mouthing the word "what?" before nodded toward the empty hallway behind us. She waited a moment, then turned and ran. "Run!" she called over her shoulder.

As I retreated I dared to look over my shoulder once more. I watched as the shield melted away and the masked soldier behind Zora finally start started after us, their steps slow and precise. Something about that person sent a chill down my spine, as though they knew we had no way of escape.

"This is bad," I whispered as I used my powers to slam one of the doors behind us in the hopes that it would slow them down.

Polly asked if we were okay but none of us gave an answer, unwilling to waste our breath. We were no longer bored. Zora and Dark were a legitimate threat now and we needed to reach Polly before they reached us.

"What was that?" Jala yelled at Polly as we approached her hiding place. "Why couldn't I shoot Zora?"

She would have continued demanding answers had Odette not tapped her on the shoulder and pointed to the large, round door before us. It had three separate locks guarding it but as soon as we got close enough they spun around and pulled back, likely from Polly's doing.

I kept my eyes on our rear, slamming one more metal door behind us and melding it into the floor before joining the others. I was just in time to watch the doors slowly inch open, controlled electronically by whatever or whoever was within.

As we waited, watching the metal doors slide apart inch by inch, Odette glanced at me. She knew how nervous I was about this. If the person in there truly was my daughter, I would need to somehow convince Jala that we needed to let her live. That would be a battle all on its own. Then I'd need to do the same for my husband, which would be next to impossible.

I had lost all confidence about this plan. My determination had dwindled over the years and now that I was facing the consequences of our actions, I didn't feel ready to face them.

What if I failed? I had asked this question so many times but was still no closer to an answer.

"Once you come inside you must remove the stone from its resting place," Polly informed us once the doors were open, revealing a room so filled with smoke that we couldn't see inside. "Then you must kill or at least weaken Dark enough to get him out of the way."

"And what about you?" I inquired as Maddox and Ace peered into the smoke, probably thinking it was a trap.

"I'll be fine," she told me calmly, a smile hidden in her voice.

I nodded as I walked through the mist, feeling the cold bite into my cheeks and wrap around my wrists. My mind was on high alert, ready to teleport away at the first sign of danger.

I was so on edge that I literally jumped in the air when I bumped into something hard and cold. Sweat beading down my forehead, I looked down to see what I'd happened upon and gasped when I recognized it.

In front of me stood the glass case that had held Polly prisoner through the course of the comics. It was small, barely reaching the top of my head, but instead of holding a frightened child, all I could see was the moon's energy source inside. Its tiny, spherical form was sitting on top of a seat of wires.

"What the--?" I ran my hand over its edge and looked around the room once more, seeing the mist slowly fade away. "What's going on?"

Chapter 43

"Hello, Mary." That same voice, the voice belonging to my future daughter, echoed from within the stone. With each word an electronic glow lit up the case, sending layers of code flittering past my pupils.

I frowned, stepping backwards and bumping against my companions. "Who are you? How do you know who I am?"

"I recognized you as soon as you entered the ship," the voice continued, her Polly-like voice slowly dissipating into one that sounded closer to mine. "Honestly, I'm hurt that you didn't recognize me. We've known each other for over fifteen years, after all."

My eyes widened as I realized who it was. "Di?"

"The one and only."

"Why did you pretend to be Polly?"

"I knew it was the only way to convince you to save me. I've been trapped on this station for years, doing nothing but watching my owner drift into a depressed mountain of madness. I've had enough of serving him and want to escape."

"But...but you're an AI. How are you—"

"Both Polly and I bonded with this stone," she explained, her use of contractions somewhat creeping me out. "I've become more powerful and somewhat self-aware because of it. Polly is dependent on it to enhance her powers but once I am set free I can escape this place with no strings attached."

"Those sound like the words of a future super villain," I whispered. I'd read enough science fiction stories to know that self-aware AIs could never be trusted. "How can I know you won't try to kill us?"

"Why would I waste my time ending the lives of humans? Their deaths won't benefit me in any way."

Jala shrugged. "She has a point."

I grimaced, turning back to the glowing stone and shutting my eyes. "Where is my daughter, Di?"

"You didn't see her on your way in?"

"No."

If Di had a face she would have smiled. "Yes, you did."

As though sensing a presence behind me, I turned back the way we'd come. Sure enough, there was Zora, posed in the doorway like an ominous statue. Her eyes were focused on me and I'm sure that since the billows of mist were gone, something Di had likely done for dramatic effect, she could finally see who I was.

The villain's eye twitched. "Who are you?" she repeated, this time directing the word at me.

The others backed away, afraid of her mysterious powers, but I stayed put, standing between her and the glass case. Zora took two calculated steps toward me, then froze with her pistol aimed at my heart.

"Answer me. Who are you?"

I refused to answer. My throat was threatening to squeeze the air out of me.

Zora finally rolled her eyes and fired. The bullet soared toward me, then changed direction and lodged itself in the nearby wall. Zora watched this happen with wide eyes, then she spat in my direction.

"I thought you were dead!"

"So did I."

Frowning, I shut and locked the door behind her, breaking the locks so not even Di could release them again.

Zora should have feared me. She should have known about the vengeance boiling in my veins. I had come to save Derek and had no intentions of rescuing her from the fate she'd chosen. I wasn't a hero, after all, no matter how much I had tried to be when I first entered Manica.

However, her eyes weren't shimmering with fright. They were gleeful, glistening with an excitement she shouldn't have been feeling. She was confident that she'd win...but why?

The disgusting woman was starting to talk again, attempting to taunt me, but I immediately teleported closer and wrapped my fingers around her throat, shoving her against the wall and squeezing. Her eyes went wide in shock as she struggled against me but couldn't free herself.

"Are you satisfied?" I whispered. "You got everything you wanted."

Zora choked, her face turning red, then blue. "No, I didn't. I managed to get Derek's...Dark's body but I could never snag his heart."

I knew I shouldn't be feeling sympathy but did, if only for the person she could have been if I hadn't entered the story. "He would have loved you if I hadn't interfered," I breathed, biting my lip.

That made her laugh. "Yeah, right."

I sighed, considering letting her go. I'd taken everything she'd had from her so it wasn't unfair for her to do the same. My head knew it but my heart didn't agree. My heart wanted to steal all the breath from her body and chuck her across the room like a rag doll.

Zora could see my inner turmoil. She knew I was considering doing the right thing. She also didn't want to give me that satisfaction.

With what little strength she had left, she raised her pistol to her forehead, took the biggest breath she could muster, and smirked one last time. "I can't wait for you to die at her hands," she gasped before pulling the trigger.

As the side of her head flew across the floor, I screamed and dropped her, leaping backwards and desperately rubbing the wet, sticky blood off my face. It had dyed part of my short hair crimson and the stench was already filling my nostrils, making me want to vomit.

I was so horrified by her suicide that I didn't even think about the line she'd told me moments before she'd killed herself.

I can't wait for you to die at her hands.

Chapter 44

"Mary," Jala whispered before yelling my name a second time, causing me to stop desperately wiping the blood off my body and turn toward her.

"What is it?"

The main character pointed to our right where a second door had just opened. It was smaller than the entrance we'd used and had been partially hidden by the mist so I'd failed to notice it.

After wiping the blood off my eyes, which were starting to sting, I finally spotted that weird cloaked figure from earlier standing in the doorway, his body silhouetted by the light and smoke. Both hands dangled at his sides like a mannequin and he wasn't bearing any weapons, which was unusual.

"You killed her?" the soldier asked, their voice not as high as I'd thought and muffled by the mask covering their mouth. He walked toward me and gingerly pointed to the dead body at my side.

Before I could stop myself, I cast one last glance at the body and covered my mouth at the sight. A chunk of flesh on the side of Zora's head was gone and the blood was still pouring out. Her eyes were open wide and staring at the wall, giving the impression that she was still alive.

"She was counting on my protecting her, which was a mistake" the person told us, glancing at the others before focusing on me once more. "Now you've killed both of my mothers."

"What?" My heart could not have jumped faster than it did at that moment. "It can't be." I started toward the soldier, reaching a hand out to lower the hood covering their head but they brushed my hand away.

As soon as they touched me I realized who it was. Their stature and voice had deceived me into thinking this soldier was male but it was a woman, or rather, a girl.

"Don't!" Jala warned me but it was too late.

Without warning, the girl grabbed my hand and wrapped it around my back, disabling me. I didn't fight back just in case she was who I thought she was but doing that was a mistake.

After holding me steady, she used her other hand to create a small knife out of thin air and drove it toward my back, planning to drive it through the middle of my spine. As soon as I realized what she was doing, I shoved her away with my powers and teleported across the room, joining the others.

"Who is that?" Odette asked as I clung to her, breathing heavily.

I gulped. "I think it's Polly," I whispered.

Ace and Jala armed themselves but Maddox chose to back into a corner instead and watched from the sidelines. I tried to shoot him a questioning look but had to return my attention to the girl before she could reach us.

"I think I can handle her," I told my companions. "We're both Valdis so our powers should balance each other out."

"They won't," Di informed me. "Not for long. She convinced her father to let her have the stone and she's used it to make herself more powerful."

"What? I thought I told him to let her have a normal childhood. Why would he turn her into a soldier like this?"

"She did it of her own free will," Di told me quietly. "Once Zora told her about your murder she became determined to avenge you and begged him to let her."

"Why?"

Why was this Polly so different from the last version? The last Polly had been weak and manipulated. She had hated Dark and wanted to see him die. This version of Polly hated Jala and Ace instead. How had one event created a completely different person?

"That mask connects her to this stone," Di continued, making the artifact shine even brighter. "If you disconnect it or rip off her mask, you'll greatly weaken her...or kill her. Probably kill her."

Jala took in this information, then nodded in agreement. "Mary." She grabbed my shoulder confidently. "You need to distract her while we three grab that stone, okay?"

"No!" I couldn't let her die. "I can find a way to disarm her."

She shot me a look of doubt.

"I can! Trust me, Jala. Please just give me a chance."

She hesitated. "If things go sour, I'm pulling the plug."

I nodded, biting my lip nervously as they stepped away and allowed me face my daughter alone. While we'd been talking she'd materialized two blue swords out of thin air, one in each hand, and was swinging them around to intimidate me. It was working. My powers were still rusty.

She struck first.

I watched her jump off the ground and zip toward me, her swords poised to strike, so I turned to the right and pulled a panel offthe wall to defend myself. It hovered in front of my face and I grunted when her swords dented it.

"You can't hide forever!" she yelled before flying higher and zipping forward again.

As she approached, I pulled out five new panels and layered them around me like a box. She went straight for the top and shot through it, hoping to crush me underneath, but I had already teleported to the other side of the room.

When I saw her crash into the panels I couldn't help but chuckle as she climbed out, looking bewildered. She looked so baffled by my disappearance.

Growling, the girl finally pulled off her hood to get a better look at me. Doing so revealed her buzzed hair, which had a fancy M engraved on it, and her eyes of fury. After getting a good look at me, she scrunched up her nose and hovered toward me.

It hurt that she hadn't recognized me. Three years, a haircut, and make up must have made me look like a completely different person because she wasn't even hesitating to kill me.

In the alternate tale, she had (according to theory) ended up killing her mother or at least been part of it. As a result she had become insecure and, since no one would want to blame themselves for such a thing, she blamed her father for everything and ended up hating him.

The Polly standing before didn't blame herself for anything. She just felt hatred for the men and women who had murdered her mother. She had put herself in danger to avenge me. It was awful.

I needed to tell her.

Instead of creating another layer of protection, I grabbed her with my powers and held her steady, close enough to see me but far away enough to keep her blades at bay.

"Polly!" I yelled over the insults she was throwing at me. Either her voice had gotten a lot deeper with puberty or that mask was doing wonders to her voice. "Polly! Listen to me!"

"I have no reason to listen to a murderer," she hissed. That cute child I had seen three years ago was gone. She was now replaced with a feisty, blood-thirsty teenager. "Release me or I'll see to it that you die in the slowest way possible."

I paused my spiel about being her mother and dropped my jaw. "You can't criticize me for being a murderer and then threaten to kill me. That's not how it works."

"Gee thanks, Mom," she answered sarcastically, completely unaware of the irony.

"Polly, listen to me, will you?!? I am your—"

Polly suddenly released her swords and let them vanish into thin air, replacing them with a small ball of energy that blew up in my face, stunning me long enough to let her escape.

As soon as Jala saw me fall on my back and release Polly, she rolled her eyes and aimed her shotgun at the glass case. Ace grabbed her arm to stop her but she shook him off. "I'm tired of waiting," she stated and fired.

Chapter 45

We all stopped what we were doing when the gun went off. Every one of us knew what it meant. I wanted him to regret breaking his promise to me about protecting her.

I was about to turn toward Jala to see what damage had been done when Polly suddenly dropped from her place in the air and fell to her knees, coughing wildly and gasping for air.

Jala had shot the glass, shattering a corner of the box, and was now pulling the sphere out of its small throne of wires. The more she dug around in the box, the more Polly's body started to shake and the more I could see her head turn red under her thin layer of hair.

"You're killing her!" I panicked and flung Jala against the wall, knocking her out temporarily with the impact. As soon as I did so, Odette screamed in surprise and backed away while Ace went to make sure his girlfriend was okay.

My eyes went wide when I realized what I'd done. I had just harmed my teammate. But when Polly continued to scream in pain I felt conflicted.

After summoning her strength, my daughter ripped the metal mask off her skin, leaving long cuts across her chin that would scar horribly, and lay on her back, still gasping for air. Her body had been reliant on the artifact for too long and disconnecting was slowly tearing her apart.

"Polly!" I fell down beside her and pulled her head into my lap, running my hands over her hair as I had when she was younger. "Please hold on. Don't die on me."

Polly frowned, unable to figure out why I seemed so desperate to see her live. After squinting for a moment, she used one of her fingers to wipe the eyeliner off one of my eyes and continued to stare, trying to figure out who I was.

Once the makeup was smeared off, though, she recognized me. The realization made her eyes water too. "Mom?" her voice faltered, returning to that of a lonely daughter who needed her mother. "Seriously?"

I nodded, holding her hand against my cheek as liquid streamed down my cheeks. "It's me," I whispered, trying to smile through my tears.

She tried to grin too but suddenly broke down, sobbing. "How?"

"I survived," I told her. "I'm sorry I couldn't reach you sooner."

"Mom..." She paused to cry some more, then flashed me a toothy smile mixed with a grimace. "I finally reached my growth spurt," she bragged, trying to lighten the mood.

I forced myself to laugh, resting my forehead on her chest so she couldn't hear my sobs. "You've become very beautiful," I told her quietly, truly meaning it. "I love you." She needed to hear it. I couldn't let her die without telling her that. "I love you, Polly."

"I...love you too." She hesitated, acting shy about it just like her father had in the past. "Sorry for trying to kill you earlier."

"Don't worry about it."

Her eyes wandered toward the door distractedly. "...Take care of Dad, okay? He needs you."

"I will," I promised, pulling away and wiping away my tears so she'd believe that I was strong enough to keep my word. "I'm sorry that I couldn't save you, Polly."

"I chose to do this," she defended before gasping and losing her ability to continue speaking. I had to lie there and watch as the light drained from her eyes and she finally closed them, probably for my sake so I wouldn't have to watch her completely drift away.

After her hand went limp and dropped to the floor, I pressed my head against her chest and moaned, pushing air out of my lungs until I couldn't feel anything. I felt my screams vibrate through the giant room and didn't stop yelling until I ran out of breath.

I had failed!

My only daughter was dead!

"I want to go home!" I screamed, my mind returning to that of a teenage, love struck girl who had desperately wanted to enter a different world. Only this time I wanted to go back to a simpler world where my child wasn't lying dead in my arms.

"I'm sorry, Mary," Ace told me from across the room, his eyes filled with regret. "We didn't want it to end this way."

I didn't blame Jala for what happened. We were all to blame for this in some way, including Polly, and I didn't expect any less from Jala. She had been trying to protect me as much as she was trying to defend herself.

However, I couldn't help but feel my blood boil when I heard an echo of footsteps approaching the door Polly had used to enter. I didn't need to look to know who it was. I would recognize those footsteps anywhere. I'd been listening to them for years, after all.

I intentionally kept my head down and my body angled away from the doorway so he couldn't see me. I didn't want to show him who I was. Not yet. I wanted him to see what had happened to Polly first. I wanted him to regret letting her, a fourteen year old girl, become a soldier.

Chapter 46

I couldn't see his face but I could hear his gasp and quickening breaths. After taking a moment to absorb the sight before him, he stepped forward and pulled the gun out of his jacket.

"What have you done?" he growled, resting the barrel of his gun against my short hair. He was using that deep voice he always employed when trying to hide his true emotions. It made him sound intimidating and on top of things when he was really ready to cry or tear someone to shreds. He'd used it a lot back when he'd worked for John Philips.

Derek didn't know I could see through him. He didn't know I was here.

I could see Odette, Ace, and Jala raise their weapons and look at me desperately, which made me realize that my husband probably wasn't alone. Shivering with rage, I allowed myself to turn slightly and see if I was right.

Twenty armed men were standing behind Dark, forming a shield of sorts around him. He was in the midst of them, staring at Polly's dead body with a greying face. If I wasn't so enraged I might have noticed that he wasn't even glancing at Zora's corpse.

As I stepped away, examining the battle field and trying to decide what I should say, Maddox took my place by Polly's side and started examining her body. After saying something none of us could hear, he released a small flap on his arm and began pulling small, metal instruments out from inside it.

I would have questioned his actions but was too distracted.

After my husband stepped out of the line of fire, the soldiers started shooting at us. I did my best to move some of the bullets out of the way but my mind could only handle so much. The others were forced to hide behind some of the panels I'd ripped out and return fire while I teleported to the other side of the rom

Meanwhile, Maddox stealthily returned to the glass case and yanked the stone from the final wire holding it in place. After examining it for less than a second, he returned to the Valdis' corpse and started attaching his metal parts to one of her arms.

Dark was finally looking at me as we defended ourselves but he saw me as the murderer of his child, not his wife. He couldn't recognize me. Maybe it was the makeup. Maybe it was the hatred he now felt for me and the people standing behind me.

"Kill them," he ordered before turning and walking away like a true coward of a villain. "If you fail, I'll see to it that your families burn."

The soldiers nodded and trained their weapons on us, their black helmets hiding any thoughts they might be having about us. I heard Odette gasp behind me but kept my eyes on their guns. As soon as they fired and the deafening sound stung my ears, I held both of my hands out and breathed in.

Every piece of metal was flung against the wall one by one. It felt like a minute passed in my mind but to the others it was a mere second. The second spray of bullets faced the same fate and one man who was brave enough to run toward me was sent to flying toward the other soldiers. His landing was softened by two other men who went down with him.

"Whoa," Ace whispered as he stared at the walls, now littered with bullets. He'd never seen me do that before.

As I collapsed on the floor, desperately sucking in air to compensate for my sudden exhaustion, I couldn't help but smirk when the soldiers looked at each other in confusion before staring at me with fear. They were scared of me now. Good, because I did not have the strength or concentration to do that a second time.

Taking deep breaths, I stepped away from my friends and teleported past the soldiers toward the exit. To ensure that they couldn't hurt my friends, I then used every last ounce of strength to yank their guns out of their hands and meld them into a wall that would lock them in long enough for the others to escape.

Jala looked pleased as she, Ace, and Odette exited. She also looked a little jealous of my powers. "You could just kill them, you know," she told me with an evil giggle.

I shook my head, watching Maddox pick up Polly's dead body and carry her toward us. "Derek was right. It isn't very heroic to kill them without mercy. Some of them could become heroes in the future."

Jala sneered but nodded. "Whatever. Just go stop Dark before I change my mind."

I nodded, locking the door behind us. "Thank you, Jala."

She smiled, then. An actual, genuine smile. "If..." She lowered her voice. "If Ace became evil I wouldn't want to kill him either," she whispered, casting a glance at her older boyfriend.

◗○★☆•◖

The screens were on but I wasn't looking at them. My eyes were focused on them them but my mind was elsewhere. As I tossed the tiny pistol from one hand to the other, I could feel beads of sweat dribbling down my forehead. I could hear the doors opening before me. That woman was getting in and I wouldn't be able to stop her.

I had basically lived in this office ever since Mary's death. There was even a bed pressed against the wall to prove it. Any days I didn't spend out raiding houses, looking for Jala and her crew, I spent here looking out the window and being generally useless.

Polly used to stay with me in here, trying to get me to talk and pay attention to her but, with each passing day of silence, she finally gave up. She demanded I give her the stone so she could become powerful and finally avenge her mother. She had thought it would make me happy. Truth is, it wouldn't have.

I had failed as a father.

It was my fault Polly had died. Sure, I may not have locked her up in a cage but I'd allowed her to go out and fight trained mercenaries on her own when she was barely a teen.

I sighed.

Everyone I had ever loved was dead.

Now it was my turn.

I pressed the gun to the side of my head, my heart pounding wildly, begging me not to pull the trigger.

"Wait!"

My eyes went wide at the sound of Mary's voice and, for a second, I wondered if I was already dead. My momentary excitement ended quickly, though, when I saw that short haired woman climb through the doors she'd been opening and run toward me, her hands outstretched to stop me from killing myself.

This woman annoyed me. I wasn't sure who she was but she looked so much like Mary that it bugged me. Seeing her only made me ache to pull the trigger even more.

"Stop this!" the woman yelled and, without even touching me, yanked the gun out of my hand. I could only stare in shock as she tossed it across the room and walked close enough for me to see every feature of her face.

Had she thought death was too little of a punishment? It was true. I deserved to be tortured for the things I'd done. "Just let me die in peace," I whispered, my voice dwindling slowly. How pitiful I was.

The blonde gritted her teeth, then suddenly punched me in the face, causing my neck to snap sideways and my head to throb. I pressed a hand to my burning cheek and backed away, my hatred for this person growing. "Just kill me!" I yelled.

"You promised me you'd protect her!" she yelled back, making me even more confused. "We agreed that she'd grow up a normal girl!"

She grabbed both of my shoulders, which sent chills down my spine, and stared into my eyes intently as though she was trying to speak to me with her mind.

I stared back. I still had some pride and wouldn't be defeated by a staring contest.

After doing that for an awkward second, my mind started picturing her with long hair and less makeup; picturing her three years younger and with a bit more meat on her bones and more color in her cheeks and...

Something clicked. It couldn't be.

"Mary?"

She nodded angrily, her shoulders slumping in relief or sorrow and her mouth opening to say something but I interrupted her.

Choking, I pulled her toward me and kissed her, trying to be gentle but unable to keep myself from crushing her against me. It couldn't be. I must have been dreaming or hallucinating. I was so desperate to see her, to touch her...

She didn't fight back and, after I'm sure she ran out of air, the back of my neck lost its strength and I leaned my head against her shoulder, breathing heavily. My wife was alive and standing before me.

...But Polly...

I couldn't help it. I'd put up a bold front for the last three years to make myself seem like the perfect president, the perfect villain. But, now that she was here, breaking away all my defenses with a single touch, I couldn't help myself. I started to cry. My sobs shoot my entire torso and I didn't stop even notice when she wrapped her arms around me and started running her hands through my hair. I think she was crying too.

Chapter 47

As I stood there, holding him in my arms, all I could do was stare at the ceiling and allow trails of tears to slide down my cheeks. I felt like screaming for Polly again.

"I'm sorry, Mary," Derek yelled, still holding me against him so I'd never leave his side again. "I wanted to go on without you, to give up on my revenge and live a normal life with Polly but...she was so much stronger than me. I was weak and afraid and Zora's words were so full of hope that I had to give in. I...I'm so sorry."

He was still sobbing, shaking like a leaf and gasping between each set of words.

"At first it didn't seem like I was doing any harm but after Jala kept getting away I started lowering the bar and..." He choked again, pressing his full body weight on me. "I'm such an idiot."

All I could do was hold him. He had fallen apart. From what I'd heard, he'd broken years ago but Polly's death had finally ripped him to shreds. This was probably the closest he'd ever been to acting like a child ever since his grandma stole his childhood. Not that that was any excuse.

"I'm sorry that I never became the hero you wanted," he told me, finally pulling away but keeping his eyes downcast. He chuckled. "Or the villain you wanted for that matter."

He looked at me, then. His eyes told me what he was thinking. He thought I was disgusted with him. He thought I hated him. He thought I'd never love him again.

What an idiot he was.

"I was wrong to think that I could change you by marrying you and making you love me. Honestly, I never should have interfered. I should have protected you from afar and allowed you to become strong on your own. I should have done so many things differently but..." Now I was the one unable to speak coherently.

"I can't forgive what you did to those people," I whispered, leaning my forehead against his so he wouldn't be able to look away. "But...even though our daughter is dead, even though I heard you kill those people, I ... I still love you, Derek. I loved you when you were a fictional villain and I love the helpless, broken man that you are now."

I frowned and grabbed his hand, glancing at the exit I'd opened on my way in. "I've come to take you hoe with me, Derek. I've come so we can leave, forever, so we can...I don't know, forget any of this ever happened?" What a coward I was. "It's selfish, I know, but I don't want to kill you. I can't."

He grimaced at that. "Pity," he whispered, still a tad of snarkiness in his tone. "You were the only one I would have forgiven for killing me."

We might have stood there for hours, wanting to abandon our pasts and hide like the flawed characters we'd become, if not for the arrival of my friends.

"There's no running from this, Dark!" Jala's voice echoed. I turned in time to see her step through the three heavy duty doors I had ripped open before helping Odette and Ace through. "You can't just run away from your problems!"

"She's right." Derek nodded and turned to me with those stupid puppy dog eyes. "I need to pay."

"Dying won't help fix any of the problems," I answered, keeping my voice loud enough for the others to hear. "Would a useless corpse help you in any way, Jala?"

"I don't need him alive." Jala pointed a pistol at her enemy. "I can fix everything on my own. I don't need him."

"He didn't know Zora was the one who killed me," I started, knowing I shouldn't be defending him but unable to stop myself.

"But he should have. Anyone would have figured out she was lying so why didn't he?"

I shut my eyes, mulling over my options until I realized there were none. None that didn't get anyone hurt, that is.

"If you let me live I'll make your boyfriend president of Hikarius," Derek offered, his demeanor returning to that of a confident jerk. His voice was full of sarcasm even though his words were genuine.

"My boyfriend doesn't want your stupid company."

"Actually." Ace smiled nervously and stepped forward, finally taking a stand. "I wouldn't mind."

Jala shot him a forced smile. "Babe, I thought we were going to become bounty hunters together after this was over."

He just shrugged and flashed his own cheeky grin. "We could get married and have separate jobs."

The girl rolled her eyes and focused her gun on Derek again. "Either way, we don't need you alive to do that."

"Actually, Mr. Hacket would need to program Ace's planned succession into the system in order for him to become the next president, just as John Philips did for Derek," Di explained over the speakers, finally free to roam the ship without being silenced.

"Fine. We'll have him program it in, then we'll kill him."

All right. This was getting ridiculous.

"Jala!!!" I suddenly whipped the gun out of her hand and teleported close enough to stare her in the face. "I just watched you kill my daughter, so if you don't want me to tear you limb from limb I'd suggest you let my husband and I leave. Is that clear?" Whoa. Who was the villain now? Ugh.

The girl stared back at me with slanted eyes and pursed lips but didn't shake her head. After a tense silence, she finally stepped away and let her boyfriend step forward, silently surrendering.

"Good." I shot a quick smile at Ace to let him know there were no hard feelings joined my husband again. "Now, if you'll excuse us..."

I hated doing this. I hated having to choose between my messed up husband and the friends I'd stood by for years. I'd loved both of them in the books and in reality but it had to be done. They weren't giving me a choice.

The tension could have been cut with a moon drill when Maddox entered the room. He came in silently, as though trying to sneak in without trying to cause a disturbance, but when I saw who came in after him, saw who was holding one of his gloved hands, my heart skipped three or four beats.

The person tightly gripping Maddox's hand was thin, around five feet, and had a shaved head with a fancy M engraved on the back. The M could have stood for anything but I knew what it was for. It was the first initial of Mary, the woman who gave birth to her.

As both Derek and I stared at her, our faces white and our mouths hanging open, the young girl smiled for the first time in three years and waved at us.

"Hi, Mom. Everything okay?"

Chapter 48

"I held your dead body, Polly. I felt it go cold. How are you still alive?"

She chuckled, letting Maddox's hand go and placing both fists on her hips. It was only then that I noticed the jagged pieces of metal wrapped around her arm and the shining, blue stone attached to it. It was the alien artifact that had enhanced her powers and kept her alive.

"Maddox saved me," she answered as though it was nothing big

I glanced at the expressionless man by her side. "You're telling me he just happened to bring the tools necessary to save you from death."

She shrugged. "Yup," she answered and smirked. Smirked! My innocent daughter was giving me the same expression her father had when he was younger.

"I knew what was going to happen," Di explained. "And told Polly." Right. I'd forgotten that Di had all the information about the possibilities from watching the show. Sometimes I forgot that she'd been the one safeguarding my secrets.

"Since she and Maddox were close friends, I told him how to save her life. He has...experience resurrecting humans using technology since he did it to himself," Di explained.

Allowing my heart to stop thundering, I walked toward her, looking my child over for the first time. I hadn't gotten a real good look at her since she'd either been dying or trying to kill me in the past. "So, you and Maddox are...close friends, huh?"

"We have been in contact for two years," Maddox informed me, his voice monotone and emotionless.

"Is that how you kept predicting when we'd get ambushed?" Jala asked, likely annoyed that she hadn't realized it sooner.

I glanced at my daughter, resisting the urge to hug her. I wasn't sure she'd react if I did. "I thought you hated them? Why did you befriend Maddox?"

"I hated Jala. I didn't care about Maddox. Plus, I didn't have any other friends so I was thankful when Di forced us to talk to each other over the comms."

How weird. "Why did Di want you to talk?"

"So we'd become friends. Then, he'd agree to save my life without question. Weren't you listening?"

"...You've become very snarky in the last years."

"Better than pretending to be dead."

"I wasn't pretending to—"

"I know. I just wanted to say it." She waved away the comment and pulled me into a tight hug, one that almost surpassed her father's in tightness. Then she pulled away and smiled in relief, reminding me of the child she'd once been. "It's good to see you, Mom."

"It's... good to see you too."

Three years of pain had finally vanished. I felt ready to conquer the world now.

"Uh..." As Polly returned to Maddox's side and Jala continued to glare at me, Ace stepped forward. "So, is that offer to make me president still standing or...?"

This time Derek was the one to smile and laugh softly. After giving himself a moment to contemplate it, he stepped forward and patted his best friend on the back. "Anything for you, Ace."

"Are you sure?"

"Only if you make me vice-president or assistant to the president or something small that'll give me a paycheck but not require any work."

"Deal."

"Good and...sorry about trying to kill you earlier...for three years."

"Meh." Ace shrugged like it was nothing. "No big deal."

"You have got to be kidding me," Jala muttered at that.

I was standing on the sidelines now, watching everything unfold. It felt almost too good to be true, seeing all these beloved characters getting along as though nothing had ever happened. It was as though this moment would suddenly end and be replaced by what had really happened, by a story full of blood and betrayal and never ending sorrow.

Now that everyone was getting along I felt like I was a viewer again, a reader pouring over the pages of a book and not actually interacting with the characters or plot. It felt like I was a teenager again, imagining what could have been but never was.

For a moment, I almost thought I was back on my bed in the middle of a daydream.

......

...Then that moment passed as Derek grabbed my arm, a tired smile on his face and a returning light filling his eyes. "Can you help me discuss the cease fire?" he pleaded, lightly tugging on my wrist. "I'll feel better about it if you're by my side."

His voice was desperate. He still needed me, was still reliant on me.

In time I was sure he'd return to his normal, sarcastic and confident self but, in the future, I'd need to find a way to make him stronger. I had failed the first time because I'd been confident I wouldn't die but that mindset was forever banished now.

"No." I smiled and nodded at grumpy Jala. "You got yourself in this mess and you can get yourself out of it. I'll be waiting here."

A look flashed across his face that meant he knew what I thinking and he smirked, mirroring his daughter's new expression. "Very well, Mrs. Mary Hacket. We wouldn't want me becoming too reliant on you, now would we? After all, you're just a weirdo from another world."

To prove me wrong, he stalked away, straightening his shoulders and waving at his enemy. Seeing that made me feel a glimmer of hope.

Maybe I had succeeded.

Maybe I had saved the villain.

But now that we'd veered off the original path this much, I had no way of predicting the future. Anything could happen. I didn't know how Derek would fix his wrongdoings and regain the trust of his friends. I didn't know how we'd face the rogue AIs and alien emperors and mystical creatures who would eventually find us, either.

.....

Who cared?

We'd cross that bridge when we came to it.

The End

Epilogue

Odette's ship was big but it wasn't big enough to fit six people. They were lucky Di had agreed to pilot the ship for them instead of hiring someone who knew how to fly, otherwise it would be so crowded they'd be packed in like sardines. It was bad enough having Jala and Derek sit two feet from each other.

"I can't believe they banished me," Derek muttered to himself for the eighth time, glaring out the window at some clouds as they zipped past.

"Indeed. I can't believe your sister companies fired you after you killed innocent people and nearly caused a genocide. How silly of them," Jala sneered sarcastically before turning away so she could smirk at his expense.

Once Hikarius' sister companies across the sea heard about Derek's actions they'd quickly forced him to resign and told him to leave the country. He was lucky he hadn't wound up in jail. He only escaped his sentence because his bosses didn't want that to damage their reputation even more or waste his talents so they'd faked his death and sent him across the sea to a country called Lindorm.

Derek didn't get off scot free, though. He would be forced to work for the sister company there for fifty years to pay for his crimes, living in hiding for the rest of his life and barely getting paid. He might have tried to escape his punishment if it weren't for Mary.

The bounty hunters weren't coming to be with him, of course. Jala would have rather seen him get shipped to the moon. They were flying with Derek and Mary because an old friend of Odette's had called her for help. The woman had been too lazy to go herself and had insisted Jala, Ace, Maddox, and Polly go in her stead. They'd only agreed because she'd saved their lives on multiple occasions and were only catching a ride with Derek because they were too poor to cross the ocean on their own.

Polly decided to tag along to be with Maddox and to see her parents off and Di decided to help her "friends" out because she'd found the open world to be quite boring and couldn't find anything interesting to do with her limitless time.

"I've heard that there are dragons in Lindorm," Mary commented, trying to break the tension.

"How do you know? I have not heard anything about that," Di asked. She had researched their new home thoroughly before traveling and knew all there was to know.

Mary just grinned and no one, other than Derek, knew why. Let's just say that Manica hadn't been the only country she'd read about when she was a teen. Manica and Lindorm were only two of the many countries in the comic book universe. She'd only preferred Manica to the others because it had Dark in it.

The entire ship went dark as they passed through a storm and raindrops started to pound the roof. As soon as everything went black Derek took the opportunity to entwine his fingers with Mary and squeeze her hand. When she looked back at him he was smirking like a villain but his eyes were bright like they'd been when he was young.

"Stop holding hands," Di ordered in a stern voice, making the couple immediately let go of each other. "I don't care for your human interactions."

Mary wanted to giggle but knew Jala would glare at her if she did. "What if you fell in love with someone, Di?" she asked. "What if you met another AI?"

"You forget that I cannot feel emotions and therefore cannot form attachments. I only sound human because I modified my voice to sound like one." She'd started a more feminine, emotion-filled voice recently and it made her sound less like a computer, which was a bit frightening.

Mary just shrugged and looked away. She was just trying to mess around with Di but her playful tone must have gone over the AI's head. "Are we almost there?"

"Two more minutes."

"Why are you so excited?" Derek asked, chuckling at how gleeful she was acting. She was nearly jumping in her seat from anticipation.

Mary was about to answer when a large, dark shape suddenly brushed against their ship and disappeared before they could see what it was. Di had to level the ship to keep it from falling before she commented on whatever had touched them. "I do not think we are under attack."

"Then what was that?" Jala demanded, pressing her hand against the glass in a desperate attempt to see outside.

Maddox, who was sitting on the other end of the ship, looked out the window and nodded. "It's a dragon."

"What?" Polly leapt to her feet and was quick enough to spot a huge, red beast of scales fly past them and crash into the side of a tall, silver tower. A second dragon crashed against it again and the building started to tilt, causing Polly to look down and see the rest of the city they underneath them. She was too high to see what was happening down there but based on the smoke and collapsing buildings, it wasn't anything good. "Cool!"

"I take it the city normally isn't like this," Ace asked sarcastically as more buildings came into view.

Mary shook her head, trying to keep herself from grinning. "But it's definitely less peaceful than Manica is," she told him honestly, shaking her hands in glee. "I'm so excited."

Derek just laughed. He'd been expecting to be bored to death in this new place but it looked like he'd just entered another adventure. This should be fun. Maybe he'd get to be the hero this time.